"Given that you don't believe you're pregnant, why am I here?"

Prince Finn Danelaw regarded her steadily. Liv didn't look away.

"Because I'm willing to admit I *might* be pregnant. And if I am, I realize I *will* have to deal with you."

"You certainly will."

"Don't be overbearing. I said that I would."

"I seek clarity only, my love."

"Since when did I become your love?"

"Since the moment I first saw you."

"If you think I believe that, maybe you have a bridge you can sell me."

He frowned for a moment, then his fine brow smoothed out. "One of your clever Americanisms." He brought the hand he was forever capturing to his mouth. Her skin tingled deliciously at the touch of his lips. "You could marry me now...."

"I could climb Mount Everest. Go skydiving even."

"Meaning?"

She pulled her hand free. "Just because I *can* do something doesn't mean I will."

Dear Reader,

We're delighted to feature Jennifer Mikels, who penned the second story in our multiple-baby-focused series, MANHATTAN MULTIPLES. Jennifer writes, "To me, there's something wonderfully romantic about a doctor-nurse story and about a crush developing into a forever love. In *The Fertility Factor* (#1559), a woman's love touches a man's heart and teaches him that what he thought was impossible is within his reach if he'll trust her enough."

Sherryl Woods continues to captivate us with *Daniel's Desire* (#1555), the conclusion of her celebrated miniseries THE DEVANEYS. When a runaway girl crosses their paths, a hero and heroine reunite despite their tragic past. And don't miss *Prince and Future...Dad?* (#1556), the second book in Christine Rimmer's exciting miniseries VIKING BRIDES, in which a princess experiences a night of passion and gets the surprise of a lifetime! *Quinn's Woman* (#1557), by Susan Mallery is the next in her longtime-favorite HOMETOWN HEARTBREAKERS miniseries. Here, a self-defense expert never expects to find hand-to-heart combat with her rugged instructor....

Return to the latest branch of popular miniseries MONTANA MAVERICKS: THE KINGSLEYS with *Marry Me...Again* (#1558) by Cheryl St.John. This dramatic tale shows a married couple experiencing some emotional bumps—namely that their marriage is invalid! Will they break all ties or rediscover a love that's always been there? Then, *Found in Lost Valley* (#1560) by Laurie Paige, the fourth title in her SEVEN DEVILS miniseries, is about two people with secrets in their pasts, but who can't deny the rising tensions between them!

As you can see, we have a lively batch of stories, delivering diversity and emotion in each romance.

Happy reading!

Sincerely,

Karen Taylor Richman
Senior Editor

Please address questions and book requests to:
Silhouette Reader Service
U.S.: 3010 Walden Ave., P.O. Box 1325, Buffalo, NY 14269
Canadian: P.O. Box 609, Fort Erie, Ont. L2A 5X3

Christine Rimmer

PRINCE AND FUTURE...DAD?

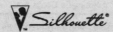

SPECIAL EDITION™

Published by Silhouette Books

America's Publisher of Contemporary Romance

Writing this story reaffirmed my joy in those two most basic and important of female connections: with our sisters and with our moms. So this one's for my own sister, B. J. Jordan, and my dear mom, Auralee Smith.

 SILHOUETTE BOOKS

ISBN 0-373-24556-4

PRINCE AND FUTURE...DAD?

This edition published by arrangement with Harlequin Books S.A.

® and TM are trademarks of Harlequin Books S.A., used under license. Trademarks indicated with ® are registered in the United States Patent and Trademark Office, the Canadian Trade Marks Office and in other countries.

Visit Silhouette at www.eHarlequin.com

Printed in U.S.A.

Books by Christine Rimmer

Silhouette Special Edition

Double Dare #646
Slow Larkin's Revenge #698
Earth Angel #719
*Wagered Woman #794
Born Innocent #833
**Man of the Mountain* #886
**Sweetbriar Summit* #896
**A Home for the Hunter* #908
For the Baby's Sake #925
**Sunshine and the
  Shadowmaster* #979
**The Man, the Moon and
  the Marriage Vow* #1010
**No Less Than a Lifetime* #1040
**Honeymoon Hotline* #1063
†*The Nine-Month Marriage* #1148
†*Marriage by Necessity* #1161
†*Practically Married* #1174
**A Hero for Sophie Jones* #1196
Dr. Devastating #1215
Husband in Training #1233
†*Married by Accident* #1250
Cinderella's Big Sky Groom #1280
A Doctor's Vow #1293
†*The Millionaire She Married* #1322
†*The M.D. She Had To Marry* #1345
The Tycoon's Instant Daughter #1369
†*The Marriage Agreement* #1412
†*The Marriage Conspiracy* #1423
***His Executive Sweetheart* #1485
**Mercury Rising #1496
***Scrooge and the Single Girl* #1509
††*The Reluctant Princess* #1537
††*Prince and Future...Dad?* #1556

Silhouette Desire

No Turning Back #418
Call It Fate #458
Temporary Temptress #602
Hard Luck Lady #640
Midsummer Madness #729
Counterfeit Bride #812
Cat's Cradle #940
*The Midnight Rider Takes
  a Bride* #1101

Silhouette Books

Fortune's Children

Wife Wanted

**The Taming of Billy Jones*

†*The Bravo Billionaire*

Montana Mavericks:
Big Sky Brides
  "Suzanna"

Lone Star Country Club
Stroke of Fortune

Lone Star Country Club:
  The Debutantes
  "Reinventing Mary"

*The Jones Gang
†Conveniently Yours
**The Sons of Caitlin Bravo
††Viking Brides

CHRISTINE RIMMER

Before settling down to write about the magic of romance, she'd been an actress, a salesclerk, a janitor, a model, a phone sales representative, a teacher, a waitress, a playwright and an office manager. Christine is grateful not only for the joy she finds in writing, but for what waits when the day's work is through: a man she loves, who loves her right back, and the privilege of watching their children grow and change day to day. She lives with her family in Oklahoma.

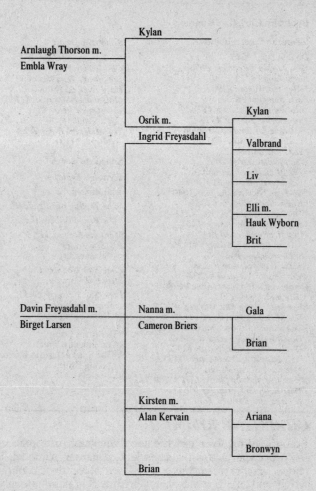

Arnlaugh Thorson m.
Embla Wray

Kylan

Osrik m.
Ingrid Freyasdahl

Kylan

Valbrand

Liv

Elli m.
Hauk Wyborn

Brit

Davin Freyasdahl m.
Birget Larsen

Nanna m.
Cameron Briers

Gala

Brian

Kirsten m.
Alan Kervain

Ariana

Bronwyn

Brian

Chapter One

Princess Liv Thorson woke nose to nose with a sheep.

Karavik, Liv thought woozily. *The Gullandrian sheep are called* karavik....

Since she'd arrived in her father's country six days before, Liv had trotted along obediently on several highly informational tours. As a result, she'd seen a large number of karavik—always from a distance, though.

The karavik, up close and very personal, said what any regular American sheep might say: "Baaaa." Its nose was damp.

"Yuck." Liv jerked away. Her naked back met another naked back. Her bare foot brushed a hairy leg.

She frowned. For the moment, she decided, she

wouldn't think about that other naked back. Or that hairy leg.

The sheep, spooked, had already turned to trot off. It had a fat, fuzzy tail. Liv stared at that tail until the morning mist and the thick green trees enveloped it.

Her mouth tasted foul. She was lying on her left side on a bed of cool, damp grass. The idea of sitting up—of so much as lifting her pounding head—made her already queasy stomach roll. She shivered. The small clearing where she lay was protected somewhat by the thick circle of surrounding trees. Still it was chilly. Especially since she wasn't wearing any clothes.

She ought to get dressed.

But to do that, she would have to move, to sit up.

Uh-uh. Sitting up went in the *not right this minute* category.

Squinting through the lushly green blades of grass in front of her face, Liv pondered the question of how she'd gotten herself into this mess.

It had all started last night. Beyond being Midsummer's Eve—a major event in the island state of Gullandria—last night was the night her sister Elli married Hauk Wyborn.

Liv licked her dry lips and wished that little man inside her head with the hammer would give up and get lost.

But back to last night.

Back to Elli and Hauk.

Liv wasn't sure she approved of the marriage. Yes, it was true they adored each other, Elli and Hauk. But what did they have in common, really—a kindergarten teacher from Sacramento and a huge, bemuscled Gullandrian warrior?

Liv brushed impatiently at a blade of grass that was tickling her nose. Those Gullandrians. They didn't fool her. The tour guides loved to point at the spires of the local churches and call themselves Lutherans, but everyone knew better. Okay, it had been eight or nine hundred years since the last Gullandrian raider had kissed the wife goodbye and set off in his swift, sleek Viking ship to do a little raping and pillaging along the coasts of England and France. But every Gullandrian knew the Norse myths. They lived by them, really. They were Vikings at heart.

And on Midsummer's Eve, they threw one hell of a par-tay.

Liv groaned softly.

Actually, much of last night was a blur. There had been a lot of that tasty, slightly sweet Gullandrian ale, hadn't there? She really shouldn't have drunk quite so much of it.

She remembered....

Laughter. And lots of raw jokes at the bedding of the bridal pair.

Hauk had gotten fed up with them—all the young, unmarried men and women and ordered them out. So Liv and the rest of them had raced down the back stairs and through the gardens and out to the open parkland where, in honor of the occasion, Liv's father, the king, had ordered a Viking ship set ablaze.

She had danced, hadn't she?

Oh, yes, she had. Danced drunkenly right along with everyone else, laughing and singing as she pranced around the ship's blazing hull.

But after that, well, it all got pretty fuzzy.

She was shivering steadily now. She wrapped her

arms around herself in a futile attempt to warm up a little.

Seven or eight feet away—maybe halfway to the trees—she could see a swatch of midnight-blue silk. Her bra. Past the bra, nearer the trees, lay the long, glimmery peacock-blue skirt of the terrific two-piece crushed velvet dress she'd been wearing. Where were the rest of her clothes?

Oh, really. How could she have allowed herself to get so out of control? What could have gotten into her?

Beyond too much ale, the answer to that one lay behind her. Carefully, still shivering, stifling a groan at the way her head pounded and her stomach rebelled, she rolled over.

And there he was: Prince Finn Danelaw.

Oh, God. She *did* remember.

She'd kissed him in the shadows of the trees. And he had led her here, to this lovely, cozy private spot. The grass had shone golden in the faint endless twilight of Gullandrian Midsummer's Eve. He'd undressed her and she'd undressed him and...

Liv turned back to her other side, dropped to the grass again, closed her eyes and stifled a long, self-pitying moan.

This was *so* not her. She was a second-year law student at Stanford, top of her class. Hardheaded and take-charge and always a model of self-control.

A princess? Well, all right, yes. By birth. But not by inclination. At heart, in her soul, Liv Thorson was American. Capital *A*. And she had *plans* for herself. Big ones.

By the age of forty, she'd be a senator, at least. Or maybe she'd end up taking a seat on the Supreme

Court. She could never be president because she hadn't been born in the U.S.A. But nobody ever got anywhere by *not* thinking big. Her prospects were better than most.

Which was why her current situation was so... disappointing.

A woman who dreamed of being on the Supreme Court one day did not have sex in fields. She did not have sex with men she'd known for less than a week. And she certainly did not have sex with men like Finn, who was charming, heartbreaker handsome and nothing short of legendary when it came to his exploits with women.

Slowly, carefully, ignoring her roiling stomach and her spinning head, Liv propped herself up on her forearms and looked at him again.

He was turned away from her, his beautiful, leanly muscled back curved to a bow, his hard, long legs drawn up against the morning chill. He remained— as far as she could tell—sound asleep. His hair, rich brown shot here and there with hints of gold, curled a little at his nape.

Even as her stomach lurched and her face flamed, Liv had to stop herself from reaching out. Her fingers itched to touch that silky hair, to trace the vulnerable bumps of his spine. He really was one gorgeous hunk of man. And last night—at least what she could remember of it—had been absolutely splendid.

She let her head drop to the grass again, shut her eyes and stifled another moan. Oh, how *could* she?

Liv wasn't married. She wasn't even engaged. But she and Simon Graves, a fellow student from back home in California, were more or less a steady couple. And even if she'd been completely free, well,

Prince Finn was a *player,* for heaven's sake. The man was incredibly charming. All the available—and some of the not so available—women in her father's court adored him. They vied for his attention. He had his pick of them and he did his best to satisfy them all.

Never—ever—would she have imagined she'd wake up one morning and discover she'd become a notch just like all the other notches in some player's bedpost. She was seriously disappointed in herself.

She was also outta here.

Now.

With bleak determination, Liv braced her hands against the grass and pushed. That brought her to all fours. It also caused her stomach to do something distinctly unpleasant—a lurch, followed immediately by a long, awful roll. She found the sensation not the least reassuring. And she didn't even want to think about what might happen once she was fully on her feet.

But it couldn't be helped. She was standing up and she was doing it now.

With a muffled groan, she lunged upright. For a minute, she swayed there, certain she was going to spew the contents of her stomach all over the dewy grass and the gorgeous naked man at her feet.

Somehow, she held it in.

Her clothes—and his—were strewn around the clearing. She had to swallow more than once to keep from hurling, but somehow she managed to lurch around from garment to garment, disentangling her soggy things from his.

She located everything—well, except for her shoes and her panties. The shoes, she remembered now, had been left behind long before Finn led her to the clearing—back there while she was dancing around the burning ship. As for the panties, well, she just didn't care to consider what might have happened to them.

She made herself get dressed, more or less. Everything was limp and damp and hard to manage, and wooziness left over from all that ale she'd drunk didn't help matters any. Right away, she gave up on her bra and the clingy calf-length half-slip that went under the skirt. She just put on the two damp halves of the dress, smoothed them as best she could and carried the rest in a wad in one fist. She did not look back as she headed for the trees.

Her father's palace—unlike her panties—was easy to find. Isenhalla loomed several stories tall, a marvel of gleaming gray slate, with a fairy tale's worth of turrets and ramparts, towers and widow's walks. It rose majestically over the parkland where the revels of the night before had taken place, the red-and-black Gullandrian flag flying proudly from the tallest spire.

Liv walked fast, through the thick copse of trees that ringed the clearing, out into a broad, sloping meadow where the ashes of the burned-out ship still smoldered. She kept her head down and her feet moving and managed to avoid contact, verbal or otherwise, with the few leftover revelers sprawled here and there on the grass.

Beyond the grass were high topiary hedges, broken at intervals for access to the gardens. Head hammering and stomach churning, Liv pushed on through the gardens, ignoring the way the pebbled paths abused her poor feet.

By blind luck, she ended up at the same narrow

back palace entrance the bridal party had come down the night before. Miraculously, the door had not been locked. She slipped through, padded down a short, dim hallway and then began climbing the narrow flights of stairs.

At the third floor, she pushed open the landing door. She went down a narrow hallway to another door. Through it was a main hallway—a wide one with an arched, intricately carved ceiling and a beautiful marble floor. A thick Turkish runner led off in both directions.

Liv went left. It wasn't far—maybe a hundred feet—to the tall, carved double doors of the suite she shared with her "baby" sister, Brit—they were fraternal triplets, Liv, Elli and Brit. Liv was the oldest, Brit the youngest.

The doors, as per usual, were guarded.

Liv had hoped against hope that the pair of Gullandrian soldiers, beautifully rigged out in the dress uniforms of the palace guard, would for once have taken the morning off. But there they were, resplendent and impassive, as always. Liv tried her best to look dignified as she approached them, an effort severely hindered by her soggy dress, her battered, dirty bare feet and the wad of limp underwear she clutched in her fist.

Not that they said anything. The guards *never* said anything. They stared straight ahead, their handsome, square-jawed Nordic faces about as readable to her as runes. In unison, white-gloved fists hit proud, broad chests. As one, they each took an equal sideways step toward each other. Each grabbed a handle of one of the doors. Smoothly they pulled the doors wide.

Liv walked through with her shoulders back and her head high. Not until she heard the doors click shut behind her did she allow herself to droop a little.

The suite was huge. The marble-floored antechamber opened into a massive drawing room done in rich damask and heavy silk, with lots of gilded intricately carved tables and an ornate fireplace rigged, by way of a beautiful wrought-iron insert, to burn gas.

Liv kept walking. She walked through the entry hall and the drawing room, down a hallway, right past her own bedroom to Brit's room. The door was shut. She grasped the gilded door handle. Not locked, it turned.

Just as she was about to push the door inward, Liv became aware of movement to her right. It was the chambermaid. For their stay in Gullandria, Liv and Brit shared a maid to take care of their rooms and their clothes and a cook who inhabited the small galley off the private living area to one side of the drawing room. The maid was young—eighteen or nineteen, max—and way too thin, with big, slightly protruding eyes in a wan, pointy face. She wore soft-soled shoes, so you couldn't hear her coming. It seemed to Liv she was forever popping up out of nowhere, startling her and Brit when they thought themselves alone. Right now, the girl hovered in the open doorway to Liv's own room.

"What?" Liv demanded in a distinctly crabby tone.

The pale, pointy face seemed to get paler and pointier still. "Highness, forgive me. Just tidying up—are you all right, Highness?"

"Never better," Liv lied with a sneer.

The maid dipped a quick curtsy and escaped toward the drawing room. Liv watched her scurry off. Once she was sure the girl was gone, Liv swayed toward the door frame. For a moment she just sagged there, disgusted with everything, herself most of all.

She needed to lie down. To lie down and go to sleep and not wake up until her head had stopped hurting and her stomach quit churning.

But instead of turning for her own room, she pushed open Brit's door and tiptoed in. After the trouble she'd gotten herself into, she wanted to be sure that Brit was all right.

The room was dim, all the heavy curtains drawn. The centuries-old rug—wine-red, with a golden wheellike pattern spinning out from the center of it— was wonderfully soft beneath her sore feet. The fine old mahogany bed, its four posters broad as tree trunks and intricately carved with dragons and vines and fairylike women with long, twining hair, loomed in the center of the room, the soft, old linens in disarray. Liv could see a slim tanned hand and arm hanging over one side.

Quietly Liv moved closer. At first, she smiled at the sight that greeted her when she got close enough to see that her sister was, indeed, in bed sound asleep.

Brit had always been a bed hog. When they were children and for one reason or another had to share a bed, Liv and Elli would whine and moan and complain that that they *couldn't* sleep with Brit. Brit was always squirming around and sometimes she talked to herself in her sleep—plus, she stole the covers.

Now Brit managed to sprawl spread-eagled, facedown, wide enough that she took up the entire bed. Liv watched her slim back moving—slow, shallow breaths. Her face was turned Liv's way and covered by a tangled mop of straight blond hair much like Liv's own.

She looked so…utterly relaxed. So totally unconcerned, lying there in her usual bed-hogging sprawl.

Liv felt the tender smile leave her lips. Brit was the "wild" one of the three sisters, the one more likely to have done the kind of thing that Liv did last night.

But Brit hadn't done it—though she'd danced with Finn Danelaw herself more than once, though she'd flirted and laughed and had herself a grand time. At some point, Brit had had sense enough to climb the stairs to her own bed, where she was now sleeping peacefully. When she woke, she'd have nothing to regret. She'd down her usual three or four cups of strong black coffee and she'd be ready to face the new day.

For the first time in her life, Liv wished she'd followed her baby sister's example. She should be in her own room, safe in her own bed. Not dressed in last night's wrinkled, clammy clothes, sick to her stomach with a pounding head, wishing she could turn back time and do it all differently.

And speaking of her stomach…

Liv dropped her underwear on the thick wine-red rug, clapped a hand to her mouth and whirled for Brit's bathroom.

She got over the commode just in time.

It seemed like forever that she leaned there, until everything had come up and there was nothing left—and still, her stomach kept trying to get rid of more.

Somewhere in the middle of the unpleasantness,

her sister's bare feet appeared on the soft rug beside her.

"Oh, Livvy. What have you been up to?" Brit's voice was sympathetic, her question rhetorical. She turned on the shower and then knelt beside Liv and held her tenderly as she finished.

"Come on," she coaxed, when it looked like the heaving had stopped at last. "Into the shower... you'll feel better."

After the shower, Brit produced a tall glass of bubbling headache remedy. Liv made herself drink the whole thing. Then, gentle as a loving mother, Brit led Liv to bed.

Out in the clearing where Finn Danelaw lay, the morning mist slowly faded away. The day grew brighter. An eagle soared overhead, broad wings strong enough to carry him far to the north, to a craggy aerie somewhere high in the snow-crested peaks of the Black Mountains.

Finn woke to the eagle's long, hollow cry. He opened his eyes and found himself looking at a swathe of thick green grass. On the grass lay his shirt and a shoe. Beyond the two articles of clothing, fat-trunked oaks stood close together, their branches so thickly intermingled it was impossible to say where the crown of one tree ended and the next began.

Finn's head pounded dully, though not unbearably. It had been quite a night. A night certainly worth the price of a mild headache. He smiled to himself and rolled over to reach for the law student, his king's daughter, Princess Liv.

She was gone.

With a soft groan, Finn sat up and raked his hair

back out of his eyes. A quick scan of the clearing showed him the rest of his clothing but none of hers. The only proof that she'd spent the night in his arms was her scent on his skin—so sweet now, bound to fade too soon.

He leaned back with a long sigh and his fingers touched something silky. Her *underlisse*. What did they call them in America? Ah. Her panties.

The small triangle of dark blue satin had been pressed into the grass beneath his hip. He snagged it on a finger and twirled it. So. A proof beyond the enticing scent of her that she had been here, that he'd kissed all the most secret parts of her, that he'd pressed her down into the moist grass and buried himself to the hilt within her.

Was he surprised she'd left him there asleep? Not in the least. Finn understood women as well as any mere man might. She didn't see herself as the kind who could ever become involved in a wild moonlit tryst with a man she hardly knew.

He closed the panties in his fist. On awaking, she would have been shocked at what she'd done so willingly the night before. The most natural response would be to flee before he woke and possibly did something to compound her distress—like reach for her and try to make love to her again.

A pity. He would have thoroughly enjoyed one last time with her. It aroused him even now to imagine staring down into her face by morning light as her pleasure crested.

Finn dropped the satin triangle to the grass. Sadly, such a moment was not to be. In fact, the night before was more than he should have dared to take. Were he a man prone to shock, he would be shocked right now. Shocked that he *did* take it, though last night was Midsummer's Eve and Gullandrian tradition held that no man—or woman—could be called to account for amorous indiscretions on Midsummer's Eve.

Tradition aside, if the king found out, he would not be pleased. And when a man displeased his king, disagreeable things were far too likely to happen to him. And more important than the possible danger inherent in crossing His Majesty, Finn didn't *want* to displease Osrik Thorson. His king happened to be someone Finn Danelaw admired and respected.

Finn pushed himself to his feet and began gathering up his clothes.

As he dressed, he chided himself for being an idiot. He should have stolen a few harmless kisses and left it at that. He stood for a moment, staring up at the clear summer sky, wondering why he'd found Liv Thorson so difficult to resist.

The answer wasn't that long in coming: her intelligence. He dropped to the grass to put on his shoes. Finn did admire a quick mind in a woman. Intelligence in a woman kept a man alert and boredom at bay. What was that old line from Chesterton? Something about one good woman eliminating the need for polygamy...

And besides her sharp mind, there was that excess of ambition and the matching control. The woman had the kind of control Finn was accustomed to seeing only in men. It was refreshing to find it in a woman, especially one under thirty years of age. Naturally, the temptation to help her lose that control had been great.

He stood once more, tucking and smoothing,

straightening his collar, linking his cuffs. It had been an indiscretion, to put it mildly—one, he had enough self-awareness to know, given a fraction of a chance, he'd willingly commit again.

However, he wasn't getting a fraction of a chance. Liv was leaving the next day, returning to America. Until then, he'd lay odds she'd do all in her power to avoid him.

The little swatch of satin glimmered at him from the grass. He bent and claimed it. As a rule, he wasn't a man who collected intimate trophies. But it seemed somehow thoughtless—crass, even—to leave it lying there for some groundskeeper to find.

Ah, to be able to anticipate the delicious and private moment when he might return it. But it wasn't to be. This woman, he would never see again.

Unless...

He shook his head.

The odds were very small.

Still the fact remained that he had been, in a second very dangerous way, indiscreet. He hadn't been as careful as he should have been—as he always *had* been before. Yes, he would confess it, though only to himself: It was just possible that *he'd* been slightly swept away.

But the chance that there'd be the predictable price to pay for such a foolish oversight had to be slight. It had, after all, only been one night.

There was surely no need to worry. No need to give it another thought.

With a grin, he snapped his fingers. There. It was gone from his mind.

Her Highness's *underlisse*, however, were still in

his hand. He smiled a little wider. A swatch of blue satin, some sweet, hot memories.

It could have been worse.

Soon, he knew, the time would come for him to make a good marriage. The patriarch of more than one important family had approached him. All of those doting fathers kept their young virgin daughters well away from him, of course. They wouldn't want the notorious Prince Finn plying his famed powers of seduction on their precious daughters until after the marriage swords had been exchanged.

He'd been...what? Accepting of the situation, he supposed. Willing to do what was expected of him. A man couldn't hop from bed to bed forever. At some point, he had to find his comfort with one woman, plant his seed, raise his sons and pamper his daughters.

So it would be with him.

And last night?

Finn smiled up at the clear morning sky. When he was old and stooped and slow, when death was near and the frost giants hounded him through haunted dreams, he could remember his glorious, wild night with the princess from America. It would help him to hold back the encroaching cold.

Finn slid the panties into a pocket and turned for the silver-slate palace gleaming above the last of the mist.

Chapter Two

Liv woke to a muffled clicking sound—someone tapping on computer keys.

Brit. Liv's sister had opened the ornate Victorian-style secretary at the foot of Liv's bed and set up her laptop on the desk within. She was typing away, her pale hair anchored in a messy knot at the back of her head, shoulders slightly hunched, strong chin jutting toward the screen in fierce concentration. Next to the keyboard sat an open bag of peanut M&M's. Brit loved her M&M's.

Liv watched her for a while. The sight was soothing, somehow: her baby sister working on her novel—*which* novel, Liv hadn't a clue. Brit had started writing novels before she even reached her teens—and *started* was the operative word. Brit had begun ten or fifteen of them, at least. When she got bored with one, she'd drag out another and type away at it for a while. To Liv's knowledge, Brit had yet to actually finish any one of them.

With a sigh, Liv turned to the travel clock she'd set on the marble-topped nightstand. Past two in the afternoon. My how time did fly when you were passed out drunk.

Brit must have heard the sigh. She turned in her chair. "Sleeping Beauty awakes."

Liv dragged herself to a sitting position. "Ugh."

"Coffee? Toast?"

Liv pushed her tangled hair out of her eyes. "I suppose I'd better."

The skinny, sneaky chambermaid was summoned and returned a short while later with a tray.

Brit played nurse, plumping Liv's pillows, getting Liv's tray arranged just so. Then she dropped into the claw-footed velvet wing chair next to the bed. "Want to talk about it?"

Liv shot Brit a look over the rim of her eggshell-thin china cup. In spite of their differences, the sisters loved each other and trusted each other implicitly. There was no one, outside of their third sister, Elli, in whom Liv would rather confide.

And she *needed* to confide, after what she'd done. The more levelheaded Elli, leaving that day on her wedding trip, wasn't available to lend an ear.

So Liv told Brit. Everything. Brit, who was wearing a pair of short-short cutoffs and a tight semi-tube knit top that tied on one shoulder, dragged her long bare legs up, rested her chin on her knees and listened patiently to the whole story.

"Oh, I am *so* disappointed in myself," Liv cried once she had told it all.

Brit swiped at a swatch of hair that had fallen into her eyes. "Oh, come on. I think it's great."

Liv sat up straighter, deeply offended. *"Great?"*

"That's what I said. *G-r-e-a-t.*"

"What, may I ask, is great about what I did?"

"Well, just that you busted out a little, Livvy." Brit shifted in the chair, letting go of her legs, stretching them out and studying the polish on her toes. "That you had yourself a wild, hot, monkey-sex night."

"Monkey sex?"

"Is there an echo in here?"

"Is that really what it's called?"

Brit dropped her feet to the floor and lifted a shoulder—the bare one—in an elaborate, oh-so-cool shrug. "Monkey sex. Jungle sex. Crawl-all-over-each-other sex. Am I making myself clear?"

"Unfortunately, yes."

"Admit it. You loved it."

"Oh, puh-leese. You're practically salivating. I don't need this."

"Slurp, slurp. And, IMO, you *do* need it. Why beat yourself up? Why not just accept that you did it and admit it was great?"

Liv slumped back to the pillows. "I can't. I hate myself for it. And I have to say it would be more appropriate if you could just…well, sympathy is all right. But don't tell me it's great. It's not great. It's awful."

Brit shook her head. "Livvy, give it up. I know you want to run the world, but you'll never run me.

I get to have my own opinions and I also get to express them.''

Liv made a growling sound and picked up her nearly empty cup. She gestured with it, frustrated. ''And what about poor Simon?'' She sipped, swallowed, set the cup down. ''He'll be crushed when he hears about this.''

''Don't tell him. Simon doesn't own you.''

''Well, of course he doesn't. But still, it's only right that I tell him.''

''You have some agreement with him that you won't see other people?''

''No. But we are very...close.''

Brit lifted one eyebrow but kept her mouth shut.

Liv glared at her. She knew what Brit thought of Simon—and if she hadn't known, she could have figured it out just by looking at her face right then. ''You never liked Simon,'' she muttered accusingly.

''That's *so* not true. I think Simon's a fine man. He's just...not the man for you.''

''And why not?''

''Oh, Liv. Because he doesn't thrill you, that's why.''

''Thrills aren't everything.''

Brit looked thoroughly put-upon. ''Haven't we been through this before?''

''Simon,'' Liv couldn't stop herself from insisting, ''is a *good* man.''

''He certainly is.'' Brit sat up straighter and offered with nerve-flaying cheerfulness, ''More coffee?''

Liv huffed out a breath and wrinkled her nose. She felt out of sorts to the max, disgusted with being in her own skin. She knew she was a fight looking for a place to happen. And Brit really did seem to be trying to keep from getting into it with her. She felt a wave of warmth and gratitude toward her baby sister.

"Sorry." Liv held out her cup.

"Forgiven. You know that." Brit took the small silver pot to the suite's kitchen and returned with it. She poured more for Liv and a cup for herself.

Liv nibbled her toast. She really was feeling better. The toast—lightly buttered with a dab of marmalade—tasted good. "At least this is it. We're out of here tomorrow. If I'm lucky, I won't have to see Finn Danelaw's face again."

Brit was significantly silent.

Liv let out a groan. "Oh, just say it, why don't you?"

So Brit did. "Don't blame poor Finn for giving you what you wanted. And face it. You had a fabulous time."

Liv opened her mouth to do some more denying.

Brit put up a hand. "I'll bet you've never before in your life got so carried away the night before that you couldn't find your panties the morning after."

Liv looked at her sideways and accused in a mumble, "You noticed. About my panties."

Brit wiggled both eyebrows. "Slurp, slurp."

"Don't make fun, please. I'm really upset at myself. You know I'm thinking of going into politics eventually. Who's going to vote for a woman who can't keep track of her own underwear? It's not…confidence-inspiring."

Brit raised both hands then, palms out. "Okay,

okay. Have it your way. What you did is horrible and disgusting and if you hide out here in your room like a big, fat coward, you might not have to see Finn again. And while we're on the subject of leaving…''

Liv knew that something she didn't want to hear was coming. ''What about it?''

''I'm not.''

''Not…?''

''Leaving.''

Liv stared. ''You can't be serious.''

''I am.''

''I do not believe this.''

''Whatever.'' Brit was sounding infuriatingly offhand. ''I'm staying for a while.''

Their mother would burst a blood vessel when she heard. Ingrid hated their father and all things Gullandrian.

And what was to stay for, anyway? More tours of fisheries and offshore oil derricks, of rolling, charming farmland, more tall pines and spruces and distant views of fat-tailed karavik?

More chances, a salacious voice in the back of her mind whispered, *you might run in to Finn…*

''This is nuts.'' Liv scowled. ''We came for Elli's sake, remember? We swore to Mom we'd fly right home after the wedding. Father agreed to that.''

''So?''

''So it's after the wedding. Time for you and me to keep our word to our mother and go home.'' Liv picked up her cup—and set it down without drinking from it. ''Anyway, I've got to be at work on Monday—and I thought you said you did, too.''

''Yes,'' said Brit, her tone only slightly bitter.

"You've got your plum summer internship with the State Attorney General's Office that you can't wait to get back to. And me? Well, I'll return to dealing 'em off the arm at the Pizza Pitstop in East Hollywood, listening to my boss yell at me, looking forward to going home to my charmingly seedy courtyard apartment."

Liv resisted the urge to nobly remind her sister that if she didn't like her life, she should go back to college or at least learn to live on her trust allowance.

Brit said, "Dad has invited me to stay for a while, and I've said I will."

"*Dad?* You're calling him *Dad* now?" This was the man who, until very recently, had given new meaning to the words *absentee parent*. Their mother, Ingrid, had left Osrik—and Gullandria—when Liv, Elli and Brit were ten months old. Osrik had kept their two sons, Valbrand and Kylan, then five and three, to raise as kings. Now both sons were dead. And suddenly, Osrik had decided it was time to play *Dad* to his long-lost girls. It had started with Elli. And now, obviously, he was after Brit. "I don't like it," Liv said flatly.

"I'm sorry. I'm staying. I want to see more of Gullandria—maybe nose around a little, too—see if I can find out any more details about what really happened to the brothers we're never going to get a chance to know."

There was a moment. The two sisters looked at each other, both of them wondering what their brothers had been like, both of them wishing for what was never going to be: their broken family whole again, their dead brothers alive...

Finally Liv spoke. "I thought Elli had settled that." Elli had questioned their father. She'd received Osrik's assurance that there was nothing suspicious in the way either of their brothers had died. Elli had believed him. So did Liv. She wasn't crazy about the man who'd suddenly decided to try being a father to his daughters. But her brothers had been everything to him. They were the children he had kept—his chance that his own blood would claim the throne of Gullandria when he could no longer rule. If someone had murdered them, Osrik would have tracked the killers down and seen to it they paid for their crimes in a big way.

Brit said, "I want to look into the situation a little for myself."

"You still think there's something...not right?"

"I don't know. I just want to check around some more."

Liv wasn't so sure she liked the idea of Brit snooping around a strange country on her own. "What do you mean, 'check around'?"

"Just what I said. Ask some questions."

"Of whom?"

"Well, I'm not sure yet—but did you know that Kaarin Karlsmon and Valbrand were an item?"

Liv didn't. "Before he disappeared at sea?"

"You got it."

"Who told you that?"

"I asked around. It's common knowledge."

The lady Kaarin was *jarl*—of noble birth—a slim, graceful redhead perhaps a year or two older than the princesses. Kaarin was always meticulously turned out in gorgeous designer clothes and she made herself available to Liv and Brit whenever they asked for her. Cheerfully, Kaarin would accompany them anywhere they wanted to go; she'd provide lively chatter and well-bred companionship.

The strap on Brit's top had slid down her shoulder. She pushed it back in place. "You have to admit, it's odd she never even mentioned that she and Valbrand had a thing going on."

"Oh, Brit. Come on. I can think of several reasons why she wouldn't want to talk about it. Especially if she really cared for him. It's probably painful for her, to go into it—and I don't see how her relationship with him could have had anything to do with his death."

"I'm only saying, there's a lot we don't know—a lot I want to find out."

"I don't like it."

"Well, I can't help that."

Liv got the message. Brit had made her decision and no matter what Liv said, Brit would not change her mind.

"Fine." Liv pointed at the phone on the nightstand. "Call Mom yourself. Now."

Brit groaned. "Livvy, it's barely seven in the morning there."

"So you'll be sure to catch her. I can't stop you from sticking your nose in where I doubt it belongs. But *I'm* not getting stuck telling Mom what you're up to because you just never manage to get around to calling her."

"I *will* tell her."

Liv only waited.

Finally Brit muttered a couple of bad words and reached for the phone.

Ingrid didn't take the news well. She insisted on speaking to Liv. Brit was only too eager to pass Liv the phone.

Liv was treated to her mother's frantic voice uttering an endless series of pleas and demands that she make her crazy baby sister come home. Powerless to do any such thing, Liv babbled a bunch of meaningless placating noises and waited for Ingrid to wind down.

Liv hung up the phone. "I've got a splitting headache and I'm going back to sleep."

Brit took the tray, her laptop and her M&M's and tiptoed out.

Liv scooted down and pulled the covers over her head. Lord, what a weekend. Elli had married a huge, tattooed Viking berserker, she herself had spent the night in a field having wild sex with a virtual stranger, and Brit had pushed their mother to the verge of a nervous breakdown. What more delights might be in store?

Liv didn't want to know. She spent the remainder of the day and the evening in her rooms, avoiding any possibility of running into Finn, nursing the queasy end of her hangover, feeling totally fed up with herself and her sisters and the world in general, longing only for the next day when she'd be on the way home.

Liv woke in the middle of the night. Her eyes popped open—wide. She was going to be sick again.

With a miserable cry, she threw back the covers and sprinted for the bathroom.

Brit found her a few minutes later, hugging the toilet—again.

As she had the morning before, Brit stayed close. When it was finally over, she turned on the light and handed Liv a cool wet washcloth.

Liv bathed her face, then chucked the washcloth toward the bathtub, flushed the toilet a final time and pushed herself upright, grabbing the edge of the wide sink basin when she swayed a little on her feet.

"Livvy, maybe you shouldn't—"

She gestured for silence. "Toothpaste," she said. "Toothbrush..."

Brit helped her, getting the tube and squirting a line of paste on the brush while Liv clutched the sink rim and wondered why her head wouldn't stop spinning.

"Here." Brit took Liv's right hand and wrapped it around the base of the toothbrush.

Liv looked down at the bristles, the neat line of mint-green paste. Doubtful, she thought. Her hand was shaking.

"Oh, Livvy. What's the matter? What is going on?"

Liv was wondering the same thing. Her hangover had faded hours ago. So she must *really* be sick now. Terrific. Just what she needed with a long flight ahead of her: a bad case of some awful stomach bug.

She looked over to tell Brit not to worry. She was okay, just a bug of some kind.

But her mouth stayed shut. Her fingers went nerveless; the toothbrush clattered into the sink at the same time her other hand let go of the rim. Then her knees gave way. She sank to the cool smooth tiles of the floor as, far in the distance, she heard Brit frantically calling her name.

Chapter Three

Liv opened her eyes. She was flat on her back on the bathroom floor.

Brit was bending over her. "Livvy?"

Liv frowned as she studied her sister's face above her—upside down and way too pale.

Brit said, "Can you hear me?"

So strange, Liv thought dazedly, the way a mouth looks when it's moving upside down, as if the top were the bottom and the bottom the top.

Brit's turned-around mouth continued asking questions. "Do you know what happened? Do you know who I am?"

"I fainted. You're Brit."

Brit's upside-down mouth formed what must have been meant as a smile. "Welcome back."

"Why are you grinning?"

The forced smile flattened out. "Damn it, I'm trying to be reassuring."

"Well, it's not working—and really, I'm okay."

"I'd better get a—"

Liv grabbed Brit's arm before she could jump up and rush off. "I don't need a doctor."

"But—"

"I mean it. I am fine." She did feel a little warm. She fumbled at the silk frogs that buttoned her pajama top.

"Here." Brit scooted around beside her and gently pushed her hands out of the way. She unhooked the first three frogs—and then she gasped.

"*What?*" Liv popped to a sitting position and looked down at herself.

Her Chinese-style tangerine silk pajamas gaped. She could see her upper chest, the shadows of her breasts. Everything seemed to be right where it was supposed to be. She looked closer.

Liv felt her mouth drop open. "Omigod."

Beside her, Brit said in an awed whisper, "My sentiments exactly."

Liv met her sister's astonished eyes. "It can't be."

"But Mom always said—"

Liv didn't let her finish. "Help me up."

"Are you sure? You just fain—"

"Help me. Now."

Brit took her hand and half dragged her to her feet. Together, they turned to the mirror above the sink. Liv pulled the sides of the mandarin collar wide. The skin of her upper chest was a florid red—blotched and welted with a livid rash.

"It can't be," Liv said. "I refuse to believe it."

"But, Livvy. You're showing all the signs."

Liv shifted her angry glare from her own chest to her sister's wide-eyed reflection. "Oh, please. You know very well it's only a family superstition."

"Call it what you want. It did happen. To Mom and to Aunt Nanna and Aunt Kirsten, and to Granny Birget, too."

"So they say."

"Why would they lie?"

"I don't know. I'm sure they didn't *lie*—not exactly. I'm only saying, it's a story. A family myth."

"But your symptoms are exactly the same. You threw up. You fainted. And now, there it is. The rash."

The Thorson sisters had heard it over and over all their lives: The women in their family—on their mother's side, the Freyasdahl side—always knew right away when they conceived. They'd all discovered they were pregnant within twenty-four hours of conception. They knew it every time, without fail. Partly, it was a simple feeling of certainty—that it had happened; there was a baby growing within them. But beyond the certainty, there were, each and every time, the family signs: they'd throw up, followed by a fainting spell and then by a bizarre bright red rash across the upper chest.

Liv spoke firmly to Brit's reflection in the mirror. "I just don't believe it. I *refuse* to believe it. It's a family superstition, that's all—and besides, he used a condom."

Brit's gaze slid away, was drawn inexorably back. Liv wanted to strangle her. "Will you stop it with all those sneaky sideways glances? You're starting to remind me of the maid.''

"Sorry—and are you sure? About the—"

"Positive. He's a Gullandrian."

Brit blinked. "Right. And that means...?"

Liv let out an impatient sigh. "Remember what Elli told us about Gullandrians? How it's such a big stigma to be born illegitimate around here?"

Brit still wasn't getting it. "And so from that we can deduce...?"

"Well, it stands to reason that if you're not married around here, you use contraception religiously."

"So you're saying you specifically remember that he used—"

"No. I'm not saying that."

"You're not?"

"No. I mean, yes. I mean, I *do* remember." She fervently wished she sounded more convincing. "I *do*..." She looked at her welted, inflamed chest again and let out a moan.

Brit spoke flatly. "You're not sure."

Liv found she couldn't meet her sister's eyes. She began hooking the silk frogs, buttoning all the way up, until she couldn't see the rash anymore, until she could almost pretend it wasn't even there.

"Liv?" Brit asked carefully. "Are you sure or aren't you?"

Liv whirled on her sister. Fisting her hands at her sides, she spoke softly through clenched teeth. "All right. I suppose he didn't. I suppose we were both kind of...carried away."

Brit said nothing. She was looking at Liv tenderly. Tolerantly. Liv hated that. She was not someone people had to look at with tolerance. Especially not people like her baby sister, whom she loved with all her heart, but who was, after all, a college dropout who'd never finished even one of the novels she'd started, who worked in a pizza joint in East Hollywood and couldn't be bothered to balance her checkbook.

Brit began to speak. She said kind things, gentle things. "Oh, Livvy. I know everything is going to be all right. Of course, it's probably just a fluke, your having the family symptoms like this. You've been so upset about what happened last night. Maybe tonight, you're only showing the effects of all the stress, only…" Brit's voice trailed off. Apparently, she had read Liv's expression and realized that Liv had heard more than enough.

Liv spoke with grave dignity. "There's certainly nothing that can be done about it right now." Better, she thought. She sounded firm. Take-charge. More like herself. She was standing very straight, her head high. "In a few weeks, if my period is late, I'll take a test like the normal, civilized twenty-first century woman I am. After that, if it turns out I really am going to have a baby—which I truly believe I am not—I'll start making decisions." She narrowed her eyes and stuck out her chin at her sister, as if Brit had given her some kind of argument. "And that's it until then. You hear me? Not another word about it until then."

The next morning, the rash was gone. Liv showed Brit. Brit nodded and made a few cheerful, so-glad-you're-feeling-better noises.

Liv knew just what she was thinking. The rash

disappearing fit right in with the way it always happened, according to their mother and their aunts and their grandmother. The rash would appear after the fainting spell and fade a few hours later. The next signs of pregnancy wouldn't appear for weeks and could be any of the usual ones: a missed period, morning sickness, aversions to certain foods....

"And I feel just fine," Liv announced with some defiance. "Whatever weird bug I caught, it's gone now." With each hour that passed, she found she was more and more certain that the events of last night had merely been some crazy stress reaction.

Liv could go home to her great summer job and her second year of law school and the nice boyfriend who might or might not be able to forgive her when he learned what she'd done on Midsummer's Eve with the devastatingly sexy Prince Finn Danelaw.

And okay, yes, that would be a problem: figuring out how to tell Simon about the wild night she'd spent with Finn. But she'd manage it. All in good time.

Right now, her job was to get her things together and get to the plane.

An hour later, Brit hugged Liv goodbye and went off to spend the day wandering the charming cobbled streets of Lysgard, Gullandria's capital. An hour after that, Liv was packing her vanity case in her bathroom, almost ready to head for the airport, when she glanced up and saw a flicker of movement behind her in the doorway.

She whirled, a hand to her throat. It was the maid. "You scared me to death."

"So sorry, Highness." The maid curtsied and brought her right fist to her flat chest. "Highness, Lady Kaarin is in the drawing room. She's asked to speak with you."

"Fine. Tell her I'll be right there—and will you please stop sneaking around?"

"Yes, Highness. Of course, Highness. And I'll tell Lady Kaarin you're on your way."

Kaarin Karlsmon rose from a damask wing chair, fist to heart, when Liv entered the room.

"Your Highness." Liv stared at the beautiful redhead. She couldn't help thinking of what Brit had said yesterday. Had this woman once been the lost Valbrand's love? Clearly, now wasn't the time to ask. Kaarin was looking very official. She announced, "The king has asked to see you right away in his private chambers. If you'll come with me…"

Liv had been expecting the summons. Her father, after all, would want to say goodbye. She didn't exactly relish this final visit. Though Elli seemed fond of the king, and Brit, already, was calling him Dad, Liv still felt she hardly knew him. And she could see no reason that she *had* to know him in any particularly meaningful way.

She supposed it was classic stuff. In her heart, she sided with her mother against him. Liv felt he'd deserted her and her sisters when they were babies and as yet, he'd given her no reason to forgive him for it.

And that was okay with her. She didn't hate him or anything. For Elli's sake, she'd come here. She'd seen her sister married, met her father and looked around the land of her birth.

It was enough for her.

Now she could pay her final respects and go home.

Kaarin led Liv down a series of wide hallways to the massive doors that opened onto the king's private reception rooms. Her task accomplished, she didn't linger. With a bow, she took her leave.

The guards pulled the doors wide. Liv went through, the heels of her shoes tapping crisply as she crossed the stone floor of the antechamber.

Her father, tall, dark-eyed, in his fifties and still straight-backed and handsome, stood waiting for her in the room beyond. He was dressed in a fine lightweight, perfectly tailored midnight-blue suit.

"Daughter." He didn't smile, but he did, very slightly, incline his proud silvery head. "Please. Join us."

"Us" consisted, at first glance, of Osrik's closest advisor and dearest friend, Prince Medwyn Greyfell. Greyfell held the title of Grand Counselor, the second most powerful position in the Gullandrian governmental hierarchy. Liv thought it odd that her father would have the gaunt, white-haired Greyfell present for a private farewell visit with his oldest daughter. But hey. Goodbye was goodbye, Greyfell or not.

The room was large, with tall diamond-paned windows. Bookcases filled with gold-tooled leather volumes lined two walls. A huge heavily carved antique desk with an inlaid top stood on a raised platform not far from the windows. There were a number of beautiful old chairs and couches arranged in separate conversation areas, and a thronelike seat, also slightly raised, with lower chairs grouped around it, used when her father granted private audiences to those who served him, or to freemen who had earned a coveted few moments of his undivided attention.

Liv didn't see the other man until she cleared the massive arch that separated the antechamber from the main room. He stood off to the side, near a rather devilish looking bust of some Norse god or other. He wore a suit every bit as beautiful as the one her father wore, though it was lighter in color, a soft charcoal-gray. His eyes were the honeyed amber-brown she remembered from the magical, impossible, reprehensible night-before-last.

Liv froze at the sight of him, a small sound of distress escaping her before she could collect herself and call it back.

Intimate images insisted on flashing, unbidden, through her mind. Those eyes...

They had seemed to see right inside her—all her secrets, all her longings—as his lean naked body pressed her down into the green sweet-smelling grass.

She thought of her lost panties. Did he have them? Did he know where they were?

Oh, this was awful. It was exactly what she'd hoped to avoid at all costs: the chance of running into him again.

And there was absolutely no reason she could see why he should be here.

Unless...

But no. That was impossible. He would never tell her father what had happened between them the night before last. Why should he? What could that possibly get him? Except maybe the king's ire.

Oh, God. Had someone seen them? And then carried the tale to her father?

And even if such a thing had happened, well, why call a meeting about it? It was acutely embarrassing, yes. It showed a distinct lack of judgment on Liv's part and on Finn's.

But this, after all, was an era when royals sometimes cohabitated without benefit of matrimony. That an unmarried princess and an equally unattached prince might spend a few passionate, imprudent hours together simply wasn't the end of the world.

Plus, it had happened on Midsummer's Eve. In Gullandria, the way she understood it, Midsummer's Eve was the one night a year when, as the old saying went, *anything goes.*

Her father spoke again, his tone irritatingly neutral. "Of course, you know Prince Greyfell. And Prince Danelaw."

Liv nodded at each man in turn, taking care not to meet Finn's eyes. "Yes, hello. Good to...see you both." The old prince and the young one honored her with the usual fist-to-chest salute.

As Liv concentrated on *not* looking at Finn, she found herself pondering the whole *prince* question. In Gullandria, all male jarl born of married parents were princes, each a possible successor to the throne. When her father, for whatever reason, could no longer rule, the princes would gather in the gold-domed Grand Assembly building down in the capital. They would hold a special election, know as the

Kingmaking, and a new king would be named from among them.

Thus, in her father's palace, virtually every man she met who wasn't a servant or a soldier was a prince. Kind of diluted the meaning of the word, if you asked Liv—which, of course, no one had.

Liv faced her father. She gave him a big smile. "Well, I'm glad you sent for me. I did want to say goodbye and—"

Her father raised a hand for silence. "Liv, my dear. I didn't call you here to tell you goodbye."

A weighty sense of foreboding caused her to swallow. Convulsively. "You didn't?"

"No. I called you here so that we might discuss your upcoming marriage to Prince Danelaw."

Chapter Four

Liv stared at her father. Surely he hadn't said what she'd thought he'd said.

She heard herself croak in sheer disbelief, "You can't be serious."

"Ah," said her father in a gentle, kindly tone that made her want to grab a heavy, blunt object and break it over his head. "But I *am* serious. A marriage has become imperative. And I think you know why."

Liv kept her shoulders back and her hands at her sides. Of course, it didn't matter what he knew or what he commanded her to do—at least, not aside from how utterly mortified she felt at the thought that somehow her father had found out about Friday night. She was her own woman and would run her own life.

And never in a million years would she marry Finn Danelaw.

Still, she did want to know what information he actually had and where he might have gotten it. She sent Finn a hot glare. He looked back at her, one bronze eyebrow slightly lifted—cool, collected. Giving her nothing.

Her father continued, "I know that you and Finn spent Midsummer's Eve out in my parkland, indulging in…amorous adventures, shall we say?"

"Who told you that?"

Osrik didn't even blink. "You deny it?"

She did not. She wasn't proud of the truth, but she had more respect for herself than to tell lies about it. "I only asked who told you."

Her father waved a hand. "Suffice to say, there is nothing you do in Isenhalla or on the grounds surrounding it that I won't learn about." He paused, then swept his arm out toward the windows—and the world beyond. "There's nothing you do in the whole of my kingdom that I won't hear of, eventually."

"Spies?" she demanded. "That's what you're talking about. You've got spies on me—and on Brit, too, right?" Suddenly, the annoying behavior of the chambermaid was starting to make sense. And if he had the chambermaid reporting to him, spying on his daughters for him, then he probably did know everything. It was altogether possible that the maid could have been there, lurking, listening to everything Liv had told Brit both last night, and the night before.

Osrik went on, "I was prepared to overlook your misadventures the other night. After all, it *was* Midsummer's Eve and you were raised an American. You have no real sense of your true place and responsibilities in the world. But a pregnancy cannot be overlooked.''

Liv stared at her father unflinching. ''With all due respect, Father, I'm not even going to dignify that bit about me and my 'place' in the world with a response. As for the rest of it—ridiculous. Prince Danelaw and I were...together for one night. It hasn't even been forty-eight hours since then. The likelihood that I'm pregnant isn't all that high—and there's no way to prove it right now, even if I am.''

Osrik granted her an infuriatingly patronizing shrug of his proud, well-tailored shoulders. ''I had, I confess, high hopes for you, Liv. I won't go into detail about my plans. There's no point. Now that there's a child coming, my hopes must be put aside.''

The man was impossible. Assumption piled upon assumption. Liv didn't know how to answer them all. So she picked one of the major ones. ''How many ways can I say it? You don't know that I'm pregnant. *I* don't know that I'm pregnant. There is no way for *anyone* to know at this point whether I might be pregnant or not.''

''Of course there's a way. There's what happened to you last night.''

''Who told you what happened to me last night?''

He didn't answer, only went on as if she hadn't asked the question. ''Your mother had my children. I know the Freyasdahl symptoms and I know those symptoms have never been wrong. You're pregnant, Liv. I've spoken with Finn and he has agreed to marry you as soon as we can reasonably make the arrangements.''

Liv could not find words blistering enough to ex-

press her unqualified contempt for virtually everything her father had said since she'd entered that
room. While she cast about for them, Osrik let out a
long sigh. He and Prince Greyfell exchanged knowing looks.

Osrik said ruefully, "As I mentioned, this marriage is not what I intended for you. But after what
happened with Elli—which was not at all what I at
first wanted for her—I find I'm learning to be more
flexible." He gestured grandly at Finn, as if drawing
her attention to some fine piece of horseflesh or a
prime breeding bull. "Finn Danelaw is the scion of
an ancient and important family. His holdings are
extensive. You will not be disappointed in the wealth
and influence he brings you. It's not a bad match by
any means."

Liv was still seeking the right final, scathing
words. They had to be just right. After all, her father
was a king. And even a daughter had to use some
care when giving a dressing down to a king. She slid
one more hard, burning glance at Finn. He met her
look coolly, as if none of this ridiculousness really
involved him, as if he were a mildly interested spec-
tator at a melodramatic play.

Liv almost hated him at that moment. How dare
he stand there, looking faintly amused as her father
informed her that she had to bind her life to his?

She faced her father proudly. "Listen. Listen care-
fully. It is not going to happen. I am not marrying
Prince Danelaw. I am…appalled at this, at all of this.
I don't know which of your outrages to answer first.
If you will remember, you gave up my sisters and
me when we were only babies. We never knew you.

We *still* don't know you." And *I* don't *want* to know you, she added silently. "The mere fact that you would dare to have 'plans' for me is insulting enough. But the rest is so much worse. You've *spied* on me. You've invaded my privacy and found out things you have absolutely no right to know. You've taken the information gleaned by your spies and used it to pressure a man who doesn't love me—a man *I* don't love—into marrying me. Evidently, all the awful things my mother ever hinted at about you are true. You're an impossible chauvinistic manipulator of other people's lives."

There was a rather grisly silence. Liv knew she had gone too far, but she couldn't make herself feel sorry that she'd done it.

At last, her father said, too quietly, "You would do well to guard that tongue of yours, daughter. No matter what you may think of me, I am king here."

"Yes, you are," Liv readily agreed. "And that's why I'm going back to *my* country. Today. I am not—"

"Stop!" Osrik cut her off with a booming shout and then instantly lowered his voice to an ominous growl. "You will go nowhere. No daughter of mine will bear a bastard. It's a crime against humanity and I won't have it."

"*You?*" Liv went nose to nose with him. "*You* won't have it? You don't have a thing to say about. No horse in this race. No dog in this show. If, by chance—and believe me, I don't think it's so—I do turn out to be pregnant, *I'll* be the one deciding what to do about it. And one thing I can tell you right now, I won't be marrying Finn Danelaw and I'm going home today—and all right, that's two things, and I'm doing both of them.''

"You will stay!" Her father shouted. "You will marry!"

"No, I won't!"

"Don't you dare to disobey me!"

"Disobey you? How could I possibly disobey you? I am not one of your subjects, nor am I a—'' Liv broke off with a cry of surprise. Finn had stepped up and snared her hand. She rounded on him. "Let me go, you—'' Something in his eyes stopped her, just cut her off cold.

She glared at him, fuming, as he tucked her hand into the crook of his arm. It was smoothly done— lightly, with what seemed like no effort at all.

His grip, however, wasn't light in the least. It was warm steel.

He leaned too close and whispered silkily, "Come with me, my darling. We'll talk.''

A shiver went through her, purely sexual, at the sound of that whisper, at the feel of his breath against her cheek. Her own response stunned her. How could she even *think* about sex at this moment, let alone shiver over it?

She opened her mouth to announce that she was not, by any stretch of a wild imagination, his darling, and he'd better let go of her or she'd break his damned arm—but then she noticed that her father had stepped back.

Apparently, Osrik was willing to let Finn handle this.

Ha. Finn Danelaw was not the one who'd be doing the handling here. The man was a player, after all.

Not the marrying kind, as they say. If she got him
alone, it should be easy to make him admit he was
only doing this because he felt he had to. Once she
made it clear to him that he *didn't* have to, they could
come to an understanding—one in which he could
go his way and she would go hers.

"All right," she said loftily. "We'll go to my
rooms."

Her head high, she allowed Finn to lead her out.

Chapter Five

When they reached the pair of expressionless soldiers at the doors to her suite, Liv commanded, "Out of here. Both of you. Now."

She got no response aside from the usual twin fist-to-heart salutes.

"You two, you guards. I mean it." Her too-loud voice echoed in the wide hallway. "Get lost."

They didn't move.

Beside her, Finn said quite calmly, "By the king's command, you are both dismissed. Go to your quarters. Await further orders."

In unison, the soldiers barked, "Yes, Your Highness." They pivoted on their black boot-heels and marched off down the hall.

Liv couldn't believe it. "That's what you say to them, *by the king's command,* and they do what you tell them to?"

Prince Finn sketched the most elegant of shrugs. "Plausibility was on my side."

She frowned. "Meaning it's not on mine?"

"Liv," he said tenderly, "you are such a pugnacious creature."

"Creature? I'm a *creature*?"

"No need to screech."

"I'd say I have a right to do a little screeching at this point. Answer my question."

He gave her a patient look. "Since I'd assume they were stationed here to guard you, it's unlikely they'd believe you were authorized to send them away."

This whole situation irritated her no end. "Guard me? Oh, please. They weren't here to *guard* me. They were here to make note of the comings and goings of Their Royal Highnesses and report what they saw back to my father."

Finn chose, probably wisely, not to reply to that one. Instead, he reached for one of the door handles. "Shall we go in?" He ushered her over the threshold, pulling the door shut behind them. They proceeded, Liv in the lead, to the formal drawing room.

She threw out a hand in the direction of a chair. "Take a seat. I'll be right back. I want to make certain we have this discussion *alone*." She headed for the hallway that led to the kitchen.

She caught the maid just beyond the open doorway-lurking as usual. "All right. I want you out of here."

"But, Your Highness—"

"Out. I mean it. Go."

The maid backed up and Liv advanced. Finally, with a cry, the maid turned and fled.

Liv chased her into the suite's small kitchen, where she found the cook playing solitaire at the table. "Okay. You, too. Out. Now." She made broad shooing motions.

The cook, looking terrified, shoved back her chair. Liv herded her toward the maid and then urged them both toward the door to the back stairs. "Go on. Out." Finally the maid flung the door wide and fled, the cook close on her heels. "And stay out!" Liv slammed the door behind them.

She stalked back down the hall and into the drawing room.

Finn had taken the seat she'd offered him. He stood when she came toward him, still wearing that exasperating expression of aloof good humor. His eyes met hers. Her pulse quickened—why, she could *hear* her heart beating.

Oh, this was way, way disturbing. She not only had to be disappointed in herself for her actions of two nights ago. She also displayed all the indications of an ongoing attraction to this patently unsuitable man.

How was that possible? Hadn't being attracted to him gotten her into enough of a mess already?

"Look, Finn, I—"

He shushed her with a finger to his fine, sensual mouth—and reached for her hand. Scowling, she let him drag her toward the hall where she'd found the spying maid. How, she wondered as he led her along, could the mere clasp of his hand around hers send a thrill racing through her? Stuff like that didn't happen in real life—or at least, not in Liv Thorson's life.

He paused before the open door to the suite's informal sitting area and looked in. "This will do."

"I don't—"

He turned again, winked and once more brought his finger to his lips. She almost snapped at him to stop shushing her, but he was already dragging her into the room, across the fine Persian rugs to a fat velvet sofa. He sat her down in the middle of it and went to switch on the TV and the radio, too.

"What in the world is the matter with you?" she asked as the radio blared Norwegian pop and a gorgeous Gullandrian weather girl pointed at a map on the TV and babbled cheerfully about the North Atlantic drift.

With that stunning lazy grace of his, he dropped down beside her. "Speak softly." His beautiful, tender mouth was not all that far from her ear, his voice low and seductive, his breath, as before in her father's chambers, warm and sweet against her cheek.

Through the fog of despicable desire he aroused in her, she took his meaning. "You think the suite is bugged?"

He nodded.

And she supposed he could be right. If her father would plant spies in her rooms, there was no reason he wouldn't throw in a little electronic surveillance, as well.

But what did Finn care? She asked him, whispering, "What does it matter to you if my father hears us?"

"It doesn't," he whispered back. "But I thought it mattered to *you.*"

"Ah," she said, absurdly touched by his thought-fulness. "Well. Okay…"

So the radio and the television stayed on and they remained close together there on the couch, speaking in near whispers—a truly nerve-racking way to speak with a man as dangerously seductive as Finn. But it couldn't be helped. With superhuman effort, Liv managed to maintain something resembling a train of thought.

She spoke the truth. In a civil and reasonable tone. "Finn. Seriously. You have to see that a marriage between you and me would be a disaster. We're strangers, really. Strangers from completely different worlds. And neither of us is ready for marriage. You're a confirmed bachelor who until this morning has shown no inclination to marry anyone." She tried a little joke. "I mean, what will all the ladies around here say? They'll be so disappointed.…" She waited for him to chuckle.

He didn't. "I'm sure they'll survive." He took her hand, turned it over and traced a heart in the center of her palm, his head bent to the task. Then he looked up and met her eyes again.

That amber gaze seduced her. Her palm seemed to sizzle where his finger had brushed it. And her foolish heart was knocking so loudly she knew he had to be able to hear it, even over the chatty Gullandrian weather girl and the haunting Secret Garden tune on the radio. Liv had a fine brain. Too bad it ceased to work properly when this man was around.

She cleared her throat and forged on. "Finn, I'm, well, I'm on a career fast track right now. I've got to finish getting my education and then I've got to build a reputation as an attorney. I have plans for myself. Important plans. I'm sure it's not easy for a lot of men to understand—particularly, forgive me for saying it, men from Gullandria—but I've got a future, in the law, in the political arena. As far as my life goes, marriage and babies are a long way off.''

He was watching her, leaning in, listening so patiently. So attentively. He was very good at that. At listening, one on one. He made a woman feel so...cherished and important. As if he was literally hanging on her every word.

It was very seductive.

And there it was, that word again. *Seductive*. Various forms of that word popped into her head with scary frequency when Finn Danelaw was near.

He said softly, ''Are you finished?''

As an undergraduate, Liv had taken Speech as her minor. She was a killer in debate; she did her homework and knew how to think on her feet. As a rule, she won. Often, like many high achievers, she'd dream of blowing it big time, of getting stuck debating a crack team on a subject of which she knew nothing, of trying to fake it, of failing miserably.

It was very strange. Back in her father's chambers, she'd felt so strong and sure. She'd known herself to be in the right, known exactly what to say. She'd lined up her points and fired them off straight on target.

But now, here, alone with Finn...

She felt as though she'd somehow wandered into her own bad dream: the nightmare debate. She wasn't prepared. He would triumph utterly, with patience and good humor. With understanding.

With sheer *seductiveness*.

She blinked. "I…uh, go ahead. What is it? Say what you have to say."

Somehow, he had captured her hand again. He kept doing that, taking her hand after she pulled it away. And then, for a while, she would let him hold it. Because it felt so good, so right, so natural, that he should.

And then she would realize what she was doing and pull it away.

Only to have him capture it once more.

She stared at him. He stared back, the beginnings of a smile on that mouth she couldn't make herself forget she had kissed.

That mouth, God help her, she wouldn't mind kissing again.

That mouth began to move. "Darling Liv…"

She pulled her hand free. "There. Now. That."

"What?" His voice was teasing. Gentle. In the background, the weather girl had finished. A man was talking now. The music on the radio droned on.

"I…well, Finn. You shouldn't call me that. I don't want you to call me that."

"What should I call you, if not by your name?"

"I don't mean my name, you know I don't. I mean 'darling.' I would appreciate it if you wouldn't call me darling."

He considered for a moment, his head tipped slightly to the side. And then he caught her hand again. They both stared downward, at his hand around hers. His skin was so warm. His fingers were long, the pads smooth, but callused at the inner joints—the hands of a man who rode. He had a spectacular seat on a horse.

And those hands...oh, they felt delicious against her skin.

She remembered, in a vivid flash, the other night. Those hands rubbing in the hollow of her back, brushing over her belly, sliding down into the secret wetness between her open thighs...

She looked up. "Please. This is disorienting."

"All right," he said, as if he had seen what was going through her mind and had decided to take pity on her. He let go of her hand. The minute he did, she found herself wishing he hadn't.

Oh, she was thinking. *This is bad, bad, bad....*

He began to speak in a half whisper. "As to your plans for your education and future career, I don't see a problem." How did he do that, manage a tone both reasonable and intimate at the same time? "I'm sure you'll get to all that. In good time. But right now, you're having a baby. *My* baby."

She couldn't let that pass. "But I'm *not*—"

He raised a hand. "I believe I'm the one speaking now."

She pressed her lips together and nodded. "Go on."

"Thank you." His brows drew together. He looked so serious, so very concerned. "I want you to know that I do regret having put you in this position. It shouldn't have happened. I should have used more care. But now that it *has* happened, well, you see, this is Gullandria. It's a terrible thing to be born a bastard here. Perhaps you've spoken to your sister, Princess Elli, on the subject...."

She didn't care how serious and concerned he looked. She didn't like where he was headed. "Was that a question?"

"Well, have you?"

Elli's new husband, Hauk, had been born of unmarried parents. When he and Elli declared they would marry no matter what, Osrik had legitimized Hauk. Until then, Elli's warrior had carried the shameful prefix of "fitz" before his name. His childhood, Elli had implied more than once to Liv, had been deeply stigmatized, a living hell.

"Have you?" Finn asked yet again.

She gave him his answer, grudgingly. "Yes."

"Then you have some idea," Finn said, "of what it's like to grow up a fitz in this country. No man would willingly do that to his own child."

A shiver ran beneath her skin—this time one that hadn't a thing to do with sex. He looked so determined. She never would have imagined Finn Danelaw would be determined about anything

The first time she saw him—it would be exactly a week ago tonight—he had been dancing. With a beautiful woman, Lady Something Or-Other. Liv couldn't recall her name at the moment. The lady had looked up at him dreamily as she whirled in his arms. Liv could have sworn that the woman's feet had never once touched the ballroom floor.

An hour later, Liv was the one in his arms. They danced several dances. And they talked—flirtatious talk. As a rule, Liv Thorson didn't flirt. What was the point of it? If she liked a man, they had things that *mattered* to talk about: politics, corruption in big business, recent Supreme Court decisions and how they would impact the practice of law in courtrooms all over America.

Flirting, as far as she was concerned, was a little silly. Definitely lightweight. Fine for other women, if that was how they chose to spend their time.

But with Finn...

Well, somehow, he made flirting feel exciting and fun, not a waste of time at all. When Finn Danelaw flirted, it was the next thing to an art form.

She'd asked—flirtatiously—if a prince had to work for a living.

He'd chuckled. "Depends on the prince."

"Well, you, for example."

"If I did work, I would never admit it while dancing with you."

Brit had danced with him later. And much later, when the sisters were alone in their rooms, they'd agreed he was a total charmer, killer handsome, yum-yum and all of that. Eye candy. Ear candy. Easy on the senses all the way around.

But someone to be taken seriously? Someone who would ever be very determined about anything?

Uh-uh. No way.

Somehow, he had managed to take possession of her hand again. His thumb slid very gently back and forth, caressing the cove of her palm, creating lovely ripples of sensation, making her think of the other night when he had—

Liv cut off the dangerous thought before it could go where her thoughts had no right at all to be wandering. She reclaimed her hand. Where were they?

Oh, yes. On the subject of growing up a fitz, which was a terrible thing. In Gullandria. "But Finn, I don't live in Gullandria. I'm an American and in America there are lots of happy children raised in single-parent homes. Now, I'm not saying it's usually the best choice for a woman to bring up her baby on her own. But there are times when it can't be helped.''

He was doing it again, leaning in close, listening as if her voice was the only thing that mattered in the world. More men should listen like that....

She drew herself up. ''And you know, we're getting way ahead of ourselves here. As I keep trying to remind everyone, we can't be sure I'm pregnant. Yes, I've shown the family signs. But what *is* that? Superstitious nonsense, really. I will not start stewing over what to do about being pregnant until I've taken a nice, safe, dependable home test and know for a fact I've got something to stew about. And, well, I can't take a home test for a while yet.''

He asked, a look of great interest on his wonderful, sensitive face, ''How long is a 'while'?''

''Well, I'm not sure. I've never taken one and I doubt I'll be taking one anytime soon.''

One corner of his mouth quirked up—in amusement, or maybe in a sort of gentle impatience. ''But if you find you do have to take one...''

''I would guess a couple of weeks, at least. Maybe more.''

''A couple of weeks.'' He said the words so thoughtfully. Imagine that. Finn Danelaw, thoughtful. Too, too strange.

''Yes,'' she said, and wondered why it mattered.

A second later, she had her answer. His eyes lit up and his face became suddenly so handsome it almost hurt to look at him. ''Then come with me. For

two weeks. Until you know. Let me show you Balmarran, my family home. You'll love it there, I know
you will. You'll meet my family—what there is of
it, and we can—''

She couldn't let him continue. "No, Finn."

The music on the radio played on and the news-
caster kept talking, but still, at that moment, the silence seemed deafening.

Finally he said very quietly, "No?"

"Well, you have to see, there's no point in my running off to your family castle with you. Oh, Finn. I
have a *life,* important work that I need to get back to.
Even if I *am* pregnant, I won't be marrying you." She
expected him to cut in about then and argue with her.
It didn't happen. Vaguely nonplussed by his sudden
complete lack of resistance, she babbled on. "A marriage between us would never work. I mean, honestly,
we hardly know each other. We come from truly, uh,
diverse backgrounds. There's no...commonality. Is
there, really?" He didn't answer, so she did it for him.
"None at all. We had a lovely, um, summer fling. I
truly did, er, enjoy it. But really, what happened between us on Midsummer's Eve is hardly a basis for
marriage, now, is it?"

For several uncomfortable seconds, he didn't say
anything. There was a lull—in the music on the radio, in the news on the TV. The ticking of the gilded
French clock on the mantel seemed to rise up loud
and gratingly insistent.

She was just about to ask him what kind of scheme
he was hatching now, when the music swelled again
and the newsmen began chatting and Finn inquired
softly, "What will you do?"

She almost asked, *You mean, if I am pregnant?* But she stopped the words just in time, drawing back, thinking, *I will not start making plans that probably won't even be necessary.*

She told him in a tone that allowed no room for argument, "I'm going home, Finn. Today. And no matter what results I get, if it turns out I have to take that pregnancy test, I'm not going to marry you."

He rose—a portrait of purest male grace. "I see."

She looked up at him, narrow eyed. "What is that? 'I see.' What does that mean?"

In lieu of an answer, he offered his hand. Warily she laid hers in it. He gave a gentle tug and she was on her feet beside him.

He raised her hand and kissed the back of it, just the faintest, most incredibly *seductive* brush of his lips against her skin. "Necessity, Fate and Being," he whispered. "May the three Norns of destiny show you the way."

Lovely, she thought. Yet another of those archaic Gullandrian sayings. She'd heard a lot of them in the past week. What, exactly did he mean by this one? Damned if she was going to ask him.

And really, men didn't kiss women's hands anymore. Yet, when Finn did it, it seemed so perfectly natural, so right.

He was such an anomaly: kissing her hand, whispering baroque Norse axioms; determined to win her to his way one minute, bowing himself out the next. She simply could not figure him out.

And so what? It didn't matter. It was okay. Let Finn Danelaw remain a mystery to her, a tender, naughty memory to bring a secret smile now and then as the years went by.

"Come," he said, guiding her fingers over his arm. "Walk me to the door."

Finn was hardly in his rooms five minutes when the summons came from the king. He returned to the private audience room, where His Majesty and Prince Medwyn awaited him.

The king wasted no time on amenities. "Well? Will she marry you?"

"Your Majesty, she says not. She says she's returning to America today, as planned—and alone."

"You used all your skills of persuasion?"

Finn nodded. "I am ashamed, Your Majesty, to admit they were not enough, not at this point. She is too wary. I need time."

The king's usually kind eyes grew hard as agates. "She's leaving, you said. That means you *have* no time." Osrik began to pace back and forth between the leaded windows and the archway to the antechamber. Finn and Medwyn waited, deferentially silent, until he chose to speak again. Finally His Majesty stopped and turned. "Liv is too proud. Too opinionated. Her tongue is as sharp as the beak of a raven. There is, in the end, no reasoning with a woman like that." Those dark eyes leveled on Finn. Finn met them, unblinking.

The king said, "You will have to take her. I regret the necessity for such a move, but I see no other way. My grandchild will not be born a fitz. Have her car waylaid en route to the airport and transport her to a tower room at Balmarran. Keep her there until she agrees to the marriage.''

Finn felt a tightness in his chest. Regret. "She will hate me.''

"It can't be helped.''

"As soon as she gets the chance, she'll divorce me. Our own laws make it so.'' No Viking woman could be held to a marriage against her will.

"Keep her at Balmarran until the child is born. Then let her do as she pleases. Your child will be legitimate, and that's what matters above all.''

"Your Majesty,'' Finn said respectfully.

The king looked at him, narrow eyed. "I don't like the sound of that.''

"I would prefer, sire, to capture my wife in my own way.''

"What way? With Liv, there *is* no other way than force.''

"Sire. I assure you. There is a way.''

Osrik waved a dismissing hand. "Come now. Listen to your king. Distance has not kept me from watching over my daughters as they grew to womanhood. I know their lives, the choices they've made, the men who swarm around them, like bees to hollyhocks in high summer. Liv's men? Every one of them, soft and giving. Tender as women themselves. They talk with her of changing the world—and they do as she tells them to do.'' The king's look turned crafty. "Did you know she's got one of those poor fools squirming on the hook of her considerable charms right now?''

"Yes,'' Finn said dryly. "Simon Graves is his

name. She spoke of him once or twice in our time together.''

Osrik strode to his desk and lowered himself into the velvet-padded, intricately carved chair behind it. He laid his hands flat upon the inlaid desktop. The bloodred ruby in the ring of state caught the light streaming in the beveled windows behind him and glittered like fire in a dragon's eye. ''Finn, we all know that no woman can resist you. As a rule, they don't even try. But Liv is not a woman in the sense that any true man can understand.''

''I know that, Your Majesty.''

The king studied him for a long, uncomfortable moment. ''She's not like Elli, who understands her womanliness in the deepest way. And not like Brit, who is wild and willful, yes, but still knows herself as a woman and glories in the fact. Liv's spent her life training herself to assume high office, shuffling her womanhood aside. And that means this may be one game of love you can't hope to win.''

''My lord, that's altogether possible.''

''You'll end up with the ashes of regret in your mouth, bitter that you played at all.''

''Perhaps so.''

But Finn didn't feel regret right then. Right then, his blood raced and his mind was clear and sharp as the edge of good sword. He knew his king, could see where this interview was going. He would have His Majesty's blessing to seduce Princess Liv. To go after her and run her to ground, armed only with his wits and his quick tongue. He would outtalk her— and yet he would hang on her every word. He would touch her, kiss her, caress her—only when she allowed it.

Until she begged for his kisses, pleaded for his touch, yearned only to have him, once again, inside her.

Until she moaned beneath him.

And writhed on top of him.

And crawled all over him.

Whenever he wanted her.

Until he said, *Marry me.*

And she cried out, *Yes!* tears of joy streaming from those blue, blue eyes.

It was what he did best.

And he did love a challenge.

Osrik was watching him. The king shook his proud gray head. "You would be wiser to take her and be done with it. In the end, you'll have to do it, anyway."

Finn said nothing. He'd already made his intention crystal clear.

Medwyn spoke then, from behind Finn. "Remember, my lord, how this situation came about. Two nights ago, Princess Liv did surrender. She *can* be seduced, and Prince Finn is the man to do it."

Osrik's expression turned thoughtful. He was nodding, but then he frowned. "We mustn't forget that was Midsummer's Eve. A night when all the rules are broken. Also, there were large quantities of ale involved—is that your plan, then, Finn? To get her drunk and keep her that way?"

"No, my lord. My plan is to marry her. By her choice. When she makes that choice, she'll have all her wits about her, else the game would not be fairly played.''

''Hmm,'' said the king.

''I believe,'' said Medwyn, ''that if any man has a chance at this impossible task, it would have to be Finn.''

Osrik looked right at Finn again. ''You're absolutely determined to try to win her—on her ground?''

''Sire. I am.''

''You will allow me to aid you in one small way?''

''No force,'' Finn insisted.

The king smiled and crooked a finger. ''Approach.'' Finn strode to his side and bent close. His liege whispered of the aid he offered.

Finn stood back.

The king said, ''I can't guarantee it. But I shall make the call. Deaf ears sometimes hear again, when blind eyes begin to see there is no other way but to learn to be flexible. And the news of the baby will help. If I succeed, you will have not only an important ally in your quest, you'll also be positioned properly, in a place where Liv will find it difficult to ignore you. What do you say?''

Finn nodded, ''Yes, my lord, if you would. Such aid would be greatly appreciated.''

Brit came breezing into the suite at a little after four that afternoon, a flush on her cheeks and her arms full of packages. She dropped them all by the door when she saw that Liv was still there. ''Okay, what's happened?''

Liv didn't bother with the TV or the radio. If her

father was listening in while she told Brit what a rat he was, so be it.

Besides, she'd had several hours to ponder Finn Danelaw's cleverness in hinting that the suite might be bugged. It had given him a perfect reason to sit next to her, to whisper in her ear and capture her hand over and over again—to remind her with his closeness of the forbidden night they had shared, to put those incredible powers of seduction to work on her.

And then, she had no doubt at all, not long after he left her rooms her father would have summoned him and commanded him to repeat everything she'd said. So Osrik knew already where she stood and what she intended to do.

Bottom line: this was *not* espionage. And Liv was through speaking in whispers and sneaking around.

She pulled Brit down onto a long, padded bench near the door. "I couldn't leave until I talked to you." Quickly she told everything—of the meeting in her father's private audience chambers and the one right after it with Finn. When she'd finished, she commanded, "I want you to come home with me. Get packed and we're out of here."

But Brit wasn't moving. "I'm not ready to go yet."

"Are you out of your mind? He's probably got this room bugged and can hear everything we're saying. If he's capable of that, think what else he might be willing to—"

"Liv. Listen. I'm staying. Our father…is who he is. And I don't care if he has spies on me. He's not going to learn anything I'm not willing for him to know, especially not now that I'm aware he's doing it.''

"But he might do *anything*. You don't know what might happen to you here."

"He's not going to hurt me. I'm his daughter, and so are you."

"Argh. Don't remind me."

"In his own overbearing way, he loves us both very much."

Liv had to admit she didn't really believe Osrik would hurt Brit. And Brit seemed so firm about staying.

"Oh, Brit..."

"I'll be fine."

"Are you certain?"

"I am."

Liv gave up and called for a car, half expecting to be told one wasn't available and that the royal jet would not be at her disposal, after all.

She was gearing up for another confrontation with her father when an attendant appeared to carry her bags down.

Liv hugged her sister good and hard. "You be careful. I will kill you if you get yourself hurt."

"I promise. I'm going to be fine. Have a safe trip."

The drive to the small airport was uneventful. And the royal jet—a Gulfstream capable of flying straight through to California without a stop—was waiting, ready to go as soon as Her Highness could board and the flight plans could be cleared.

Her driver opened her door for her and ushered her from the car, detouring next to the trunk, where he hauled out her bags and turned them over to the porter who would load them in the luggage compartment.

The air was clear and the wind was up. Liv could smell the ocean on it. Overhead, a few gulls dipped and soared. She smoothed her blowing hair off her face and ran for the steps that led up to the passenger door.

The pretty attendant—the same one who'd taken care of Liv and Brit on the flight over—greeted her at the top. "Welcome, Your Highness. So lovely to have you flying with us again."

Liv gave the woman a big smile and ducked into the cabin to find that there was one other passenger traveling with her: Finn Danelaw.

Chapter Six

Liv hovered in the galley area, the flight attendant at her back, glaring at the man waiting for her in the cabin.

"Liv. Welcome." Finn rose from the plush leather seat and held out a fine long-fingered hand as if inviting her to dance.

Liv swept through the narrow doorway into the cabin, then stopped short and turned back to the flight attendant. "Excuse us for a moment." She shut the door in the attendant's pretty, bewildered face and whirled on Finn. "I'll ask the obvious. What are you doing here?"

He gave her one of his oh-so-elegant shrugs. "You wouldn't come to my home. I thought I might visit you in yours."

"What we had to say to each other has been said.

It's done, finished, through. I will never again have anything to do with you. Thus, it's impossible for you to 'visit' me.''

"I hope to convince you to reconsider my suit."

"I absolutely will not. I meant what I said. I won't marry you. No matter what…happens."

"You won't marry me. I understand. You've said it repeatedly. There's no need to say it again."

"Oh, why can't I get through to you?"

"But Liv darling, you *have* gotten through to me."

"I am not your darling."

"Ah. Yes. I believe you've mentioned that, too."

"Then don't call me that."

He dropped into the chair again, rested an elbow on the wide, padded arm and looked up at her, an absolutely infuriating expression of charmed bemusement on his gorgeous face. "He who fights shadows only squanders his strength."

She really, sincerely, wanted to bop him on the head with her Balenciaga lariat bag. "What is that? One of those obscure Gullandrian sayings of yours?"

"Hardly of mine. And I do think the meaning is clear."

"There is no point to this. This will get you exactly nowhere."

"So you've explained to me. I find, though, that I have an unrelenting yearning to see Sacramento."

"Oh, right." She was truly furious. She felt as if, any second now, steam would start hissing out of her ears. "Prime vacation destination in the Golden State. No doubt about it. What's Monterey, San Francisco, Santa Barbara, when you can be in Sacramento?"

One corner of his mouth lifted. Lazily. *Seductively.* "A visit of...two or three weeks, I would say..."

Oh, there was absolutely no point in talking with him. It got her nowhere and seemed to provide him an endless source of amusement.

Should she deplane?

To what purpose? She'd just have to find some other way to get home. And Finn would still be there when she arrived.

She turned from him abruptly and yanked open the door to the galley area. The attendant stood on the other side, looking sheepish.

"Come in, come in," Liv said with heavy irony. "Prince Danelaw and I have nothing more to say to each other."

Liv put the man on permanent *ignore.* For the entire flight, she did not say one word to him.

They were served an excellent meal of veal medallions with pasta salad and artichokes. Liv savored hers in silence, careful never to let her gaze stray in the direction of the prince, shaking her head when the attendant offered her a glass of wine. It would be a long time before she let anything with alcohol in it cross her lips again.

After she'd eaten, she moved to the bedroom half of the cabin, pulled the accordion doors shut and didn't emerge for the several hours left in the flight.

It worked out fine. She had a bed to stretch out in and a rest room all to herself if she needed it. She watched a movie, read the new Sandra Day O'Connor memoir and told herself she was hardly giving a thought to the patient, gorgeous, *relentless* man on the other side of the flimsy doors.

She even had the foresight to call ahead and arrange for a cab to be waiting at the other end. Her father had sent a limousine to pick her up and take her to the airport for the flight to Gullandria, but she had no illusions he would have made any such arrangement now. She was not going to be stuck without a ride—not with the ever-resourceful Prince Finn around. Of course, he'd have a limousine waiting. And he'd be oh-so-eager to give her a lift.

The flight took ten hours. With the eight-hour time difference, they touched down at Sacramento Executive Airport at a little after eight in the evening— only two hours later than the time it had been when they left Gullandria.

Liv looked out the window and saw a throng of reporters waiting on the tarmac—along with a shiny black limousine and an undistinguished-looking white four-door sedan: her cab.

She scrawled the address and phone number of her summer sublet on the back of a business card and gave it to the flight attendant along with a fifty. "Make certain my bags get to that address tonight."

"Yes, Your Highness. I'll see to it. Thank you for flying with us."

Liv smiled politely and moved on. She got out the door first, ahead of Finn. The cameras started clicking the minute she appeared on the small landing at the top of the steps. And the questions came at her as she descended.

"Princess Liv, how's your sister, the warrior's bride?"

"Elli is blissfully happy."

"Where will they honeymoon?"

"You know, I can't say for certain...."

"I see Princess Brit isn't with you. Why?"

"She decided to extend her visit in my father's country."

Finn was right behind her. And they noticed. The women in the crowd waved and called to him—by name. "Prince Danelaw!"

"Prince Finn, this way!"

Finn grinned and waved. Click-click-click went the cameras. More than one woman fanned herself and sighed.

"Princess Liv, we understand that you and Prince Finn will be celebrating a wedding of your own very soon."

She'd been smiling until then. "I beg your pardon, I hardly know Prince Finn." Well, it was *true*. Just because she'd slept with him, didn't mean she *knew* him. "He's visiting Sacramento. We merely flew here on the same plane. We are *not* engaged—I'm not engaged to anyone."

"But my sources have it that—"

"Your sources have it wrong." Liv elbowed her way through the jostling crowd as quickly and smoothly as she could manage it, with the questions still flying and the cameras clicking away.

She couldn't believe it. How could they possibly have any clue about her and Finn? But then she thought of her father and decided this was just like him: to plant false information and put her in the embarrassing position of having to deny it.

Finn stayed right with her, too close for comfort.

He was at her side when she reached the cab. The cabby hadn't thought to get out and open her door for her.

Finn did the honors. He reached for the handle and then stopped to grant her a heart-twisting smile. "Are you sure you won't ride with me? I'd be happy to take you wherever you'd like to go."

Oh, I'll just bet, she thought.

Click-click-click-click. The cameramen kept shooting away.

Live returned his smile, but only because she'd been taught by her mother that one must never let the paparazzi see one sweat. "No, thank you. I'll be fine. Enjoy your visit to Sacramento."

His gaze tracked to her mouth, then flicked up to collide with hers again. "Yes. I have a feeling I'm going to be very glad I came."

Another of those infuriating, purely sexual shivers quivered through her. She went on smiling and spoke very softly. "Open that door or I'll spit in your eye."

With a flourish, he pulled the door wide.

Liv gave the cabby her address and turned to look out the rear window as the cab pulled away from the crowd of reporters. She wanted to make certain Finn didn't follow her.

Still waving at the clicking cameras, he strode over to the long, black limousine. The limo driver jumped out and opened the door. Sable hair shining in the fading light of early evening, the prince ducked inside.

Liv kept watching, until the limo went another way. Apparently, Finn had better sense than to try tailing her home. A wise move on his part. If he had, she'd intended to call the police on him.

She could see the headlines now: Princess Liv And Her Handsome Stalker, The Prince. Royal Engagement A No-Go. His Highness In Jail. It would be ugly. And he would fully deserve whatever embarrassment he suffered.

Where would he go? she found herself wondering, though she knew she shouldn't spare another thought for him. Some exclusive hotel, no doubt. Wherever. She didn't care. She was jet-lagged and emotionally exhausted and she needed a good night's rest. She had to be at work tomorrow.

The cabby let her off in front of the cute, attractively renovated two-story Victorian on T Street. It belonged to a friend of her mother's—a friend who was visiting Alaska for the summer. Ingrid had wanted Liv to stay in her old room at the Land Park house where Liv and her sisters had grown up. But Liv treasured her independence too much. She wanted to come and go as she pleased and know she wouldn't be worrying her mother. Plus, the T Street house was downtown, closer to the State Attorney General's Office and her job.

Inside, she brewed herself a cup of soothing tea and checked in with her message service. There was one from Simon, which brought a fresh twinge of guilt.

He was in town—Simon was spending his summer on the campaign trail with a senatorial candidate they both supported—and he wanted her to call him at his hotel. He reminded her about the rally tomorrow, the one she'd promised him several weeks ago that she'd attend.

She thought of a thousand excuses why she didn't have to call him right then. None of them added up to anything but the desire to evade an unpleasant duty. She picked up the phone.

In the instant before she punched up his number, the doorbell rang. Her bags.

She had the driver lug them in. He left them in a neat row inside the front door at the foot of the stairs. She tipped him and locked up. Then she grabbed her overnighter—the rest she'd worry about tomorrow— and went on upstairs.

The phone rang as she was pulling on her thick terry bathrobe. She knew it was going to be Simon. She considered not answering.

"Coward," she muttered, and picked up the receiver.

It was her mother.

"Liv darling, you're home." Her mother always called her darling. She'd never thought a thing about it. But now, the word stood out when Ingrid said it, making Liv think of the infuriating Prince Finn.

"Liv?" Ingrid asked, a note of concern creeping in.

"Sorry, Mom. I'm beat. And yes, I'm home. Safe and sound."

"Good trip?"

"Can't complain. Nonstop. The king's luxury jet." Liv waited, somewhat grimly, for her mother to start in about Brit staying on in Gullandria and Elli marrying "that big Gullandrian thug."

But she didn't. She only said, "It's a long flight, I know. Take a hot bath and get some rest."

Liv heaved a grateful sigh. She wanted to be there for Ingrid, to listen to her worries and provide a shoulder to cry on. But tonight, it really would have been one big scene too many. She said warmly, "A bath and a good night's sleep. My intentions exactly."

"And how about dinner, tomorrow night? I'll have Hilda make your favorite stuffed pork chops. Say sevenish?"

"Sounds wonderful. I'll be there."

Liv was just about to say good-night when it occurred to her that her mother might hear about her so-called engagement before she could explain the situation tomorrow at dinner. Ingrid hopefully would take such news with a grain of salt. But then again, she might completely freak. Hard to say. "Listen, Mom, I just want to warn you."

"My. This does sound ominous." Ingrid's voice was light. Almost teasing.

And Liv wanted it to stay that way. "It's not ominous. Not in the least. It's nothing. I met this, well, this very charming man, in Gullandria. We spent some time together. You know, just casual?" Well, okay, not *completely* casual. But she was hoping Ingrid would never have to know about that. "We danced. We...talked. We went riding. He gave me a tour of Lysgard. He, um, showed Brit and me around...."

"Darling, what *are* you getting at?"

"Well, his name is Danelaw. Prince Finn Danelaw. And somehow, the press has gotten hold of it.

As usual, they've made a big deal out of nothing. They seem to think I'm engaged to Finn. It's not true. There's *nothing* between us. And I, well, I just wanted you to hear it from me first, that's all.''

Her mother made a noise in her throat.

Liv couldn't decide what that sound might mean. ''Mom, it's nothing. I just didn't want you to read it first in the papers or have somebody tell you before I had a chance to.''

''Darling.''

''Mmm?''

''Don't give it another thought. I know how the press is.'' And she did, of course. After all, Ingrid Freyasdahl Thorson had been known for over two decades as the Runaway Gullandrian Queen. She was no stranger to scandal or to lying reporters. ''And look at it this way…''

''What way?''

''If they had to pair you with a Gullandrian, at least he's a Danelaw. It's a very old family. Very wealthy. And powerful—at least at one time. Danelaws once sat on the throne of Gullandria, did you know that? For several generations, as a matter of fact.''

''Mom, that's not the point.''

''Of course it's not, darling. I'm only trying to…look on the bright side.''

''There is no bright side to nosy reporters making up lies about me.''

''Sweetheart. Take a bath. Go to bed. We'll talk tomorrow night.''

* * *

Liv thought of Simon after she hung up. Tomorrow, she promised herself. Tomorrow she'd make the time to give him a call.

She went to the bathroom and filled the claw-footed tub. She soaked for an hour.

But when she climbed into the big, comfy canopy bed with the fat, luxurious pillow-top mattress, sleep wouldn't come. Every time she'd relax, she'd find herself thinking sexy thoughts about Finn—the way his hair curled at his nape, the feel of his hand wrapped around hers, the brush of that thumb of his—gently, relentlessly—against her palm.

She'd catch herself and groan in frustration—and realize she was wide-awake.

She got up at seven, ate breakfast and spent a half an hour carefully making up her face, troweling on the concealer in an effort to hide the dark smudges beneath her eyes. Then she dressed for success in a knee-grazing pencil skirt, short jacket to match, with her faux croc pumps and the beautiful single strand of Mikimoto pearls her Granny Birget had presented to her on her graduation from high school, right after she'd given the valedictory speech. Liv always felt good when she wore her valedictory pearls.

Her platinum blue Lexus was waiting in back. When she pulled out of the driveway and onto Thirteenth Street, she spotted a reporter crouched among the rhododendrons beside the house's wide front porch. The man's camera was pressed to his face. He pointed the thing at her car as she rolled up to the corner stop sign.

Liv put the passenger window down, leaned across the seat and signaled the man over. She smiled for a couple of close-ups and reassured him that, no, she really was not going to marry Prince Finn Danelaw. "And I would appreciate it if you'd stay out of the rhododendrons. They break so easily and you know this isn't even actually my house. A friend of the family's has let me use it for the summer."

Bowing and scraping, the man backed away, promising he'd never get near the flowerbeds again.

At the State Attorney General's Office, Liv spent the day answering phones, typing letters and researching a few finer points of law. She had no illusions about the complexity of her three-month job. The work she did as an intern was what any junior clerk might do. In terms of job description, she wasn't much more than a glorified gofer. She got work-study units for it in lieu of a salary.

But the contacts she was making were invaluable. One in every seven Americans lived in California. It was, in terms of the numbers and diversity of its people, by far the biggest state in America. And Liv, at the age of twenty-three, was rubbing elbows with those who ran it.

She left work at a little after six, with plenty of time to stop in at the house on T Street, where she noticed with satisfaction that the rhododendrons were undisturbed. Not a reporter in sight.

She got rid of her panty hose and changed into sandals, a more casual skirt and a comfy embroidered gauze peasant top. She thought of Simon again right before she went back out the door. She was early. She had time to give him a quick call.

But no. What she had to tell him wasn't something she could explain in a ten-minute call. Later tonight, she promised herself.

She got to her mother's at twenty of seven. The three-story Tudor where Liv and her sisters had grown up sat on a wide, curving tree-shaded street. The graceful old houses were set far back from the sidewalks, up long sweeps of green lawn, with driveways that led around back, to three- and four-car garages, maids' quarters above. Not a street of mansions, by any means. But a street that spoke of prosperity, of the very-well-to-do. The sisters had always known that their mother—not only a runaway queen, but an heiress in her own right—could have raised them in a bigger house. They could have lived in San Diego or Beverly Hills. In a Park Avenue town house. In a palace in Timbuktu.

But Ingrid had wanted her daughters to have "some semblance of a normal childhood." So they attended public schools—not always the safest endeavor in recent years. They played soccer on community teams. And they lived on a nice, wide, oak-shaded street in Land Park.

Liv pulled into the driveway on the side of the house and drove on beneath the porte cochere to the wide parking area with its row of four garages in back. She went in through the back door, the heels of her sandals tapping on the terra-cotta tiles of the service porch floor. She found Hilda, her mother's housekeeper and cook for as long as Liv could remember, busy chopping herbs at the marble-topped island in the center of the big kitchen.

"Hildy, I'm home!" Liv announced in a teasing singsong. She breezed over to the imposing, stern-faced woman with the iron-gray hair and planted a loud kiss on her gaunt cheek. "Mmm. I smell stuffed pork chops. I think I'm in heaven."

"Liv," Hilda said, coming as close to cracking a smile as she ever did. "It is good to see your face." Her dark eyes met Liv's.

Liv stepped back. "What's wrong?"

"Excuse me?"

"You look...I don't know. Is something wrong?"

"Why, no. Nothing."

Liv studied the housekeeper for a moment and then shrugged. Hilda was Gullandrian—Ingrid had brought her back to California when she left Osrik— and often mysterious or moody for reasons that Liv and her sisters never could figure out.

Hilda had gone back to chopping her herbs.

"Where's Mom?"

"In the family room."

Liv grabbed an apple from the bowl on the side counter and headed for the central hall. She heard her mother's throaty, musical laughter as she approached the open doorway.

And then she heard a man's low, teasing voice. She froze stock still as she recognized that voice and understood the reason for the strange look in Hilda's eyes.

Finn Danelaw was in the family room, making her mother laugh.

Chapter Seven

Ingrid laughed again. "Oh, Finn. I really think you're a hazard on our highways. Use a driver from now on."

Finn chuckled, so charmingly. "But I love driving, especially with all the windows down, the radio turned up loud. And going very fast. Sadly, here in America, there are so many other cars in the way. Big ones, too. I saw my first Lincoln Navigator today. Amazing. And with a very small, very angry looking woman at the wheel...."

"Yes," said Ingrid, a lightness in her voice that had been there too seldom of late. "You ought not to mess with an American woman in an SUV."

"Excellent advice, I have no doubt."

Liv, still hanging back near the foot of the stairs, straightened her shoulders and stepped proudly into the open doorway.

Her mother, in a chair facing the hall, saw her first. Finn, lounging against the mantel on the outside wall, turned when he caught the direction of his hostess's gaze.

Ingrid didn't miss a beat. Her wide mouth spread in a happy, gracious smile. "Liv darling. You're early."

"Mother," Liv said. She felt like a wire—strung tight, but not yet sprung. "Finn. How are you?"

He gave her the most beautiful welcoming smile. "Better by the moment." Oh, he was good. He was very, very good.

"What a surprise," Liv sneered, "to see *you* here."

Those amber eyes glittered with challenge, with something Liv couldn't quite define. "Her Majesty has graciously invited me to be her guest during my visit to your beautiful city."

The wire of Liv's temper pulled all the tighter. She flashed a furious look at her mother.

Ingrid rose to her feet. "Finn, I wonder…"

He nodded. "I can see the two of you would like a little time alone."

Ingrid beamed him a grateful smile. "Yes, that would be wonderful. Fifteen minutes?"

"No problem." He bowed over her hand and then he was striding straight for Liv. He wore camel-colored slacks and a polo shirt and he made something inside Liv go silly and hopeless and weak. Oh, why did he have to be so utterly gorgeous?

He reached her. And she was still standing there, rooted to the spot, blocking the doorway. She stared at him and he stared back at her. The air around them

seemed to be humming—with her own righteous in-
dignation, she tried to convince herself, as she ordered her foolish, wobbly legs to get her out of his
way. With a quick, polite nod, he went on by.

She heard his footsteps going up the stairs. They
faded off on the second floor. By then, she'd more
or less pulled herself together. She leveled a look of
disdain at her mother. "Well?"

"Oh, darling." With a long sigh, her mother
dropped to her chair again. "I hope you're not *too*
upset with me...." She looked across at Liv, hoping,
no doubt, that Liv would rush in with eager reassur-
ances, vowing she wasn't angry in the least.

No way.

Ingrid became very absorbed with crossing her
long legs and smoothing her bronze-colored linen
skirt over her knees. "Oh, all right," she finally admitted, "I should have said something earlier."

"Now there's a thought. Maybe you could have
mentioned it last night, while I was stumbling all
over myself trying to make sure you wouldn't worry
if you heard any rumors about my 'engagement' to
that man."

"I wanted you to get a good night's sleep, be fresh
for your job today. I knew you'd be angry, whenever
I told you. And last night it simply seemed...wiser,
just to wait until this evening."

Liv still held the apple she'd carried from the
kitchen. Her appetite for it had vanished. She set it
on the counter in the built-in bar area and moved
nearer the chair where her mother sat. "Finn was
here last night when you called me, wasn't he?"

Her mother sighed again and nodded.

"Then you know about what happened between us?"

"Yes, darling. I do."

Did the humiliation never end? One night's indiscretion and *everybody* had to know about it, her mother included. "How did you find out?"

"I spoke with your father. He called yesterday. We had a long talk."

Liv wondered if she'd heard right. "Wait a minute. The way you say that, you seem to be implying that you and Father had an actual conversation."

"Yes. I would say the word 'conversation' pretty much describes what took place between us."

"But...you never have conversations with Father." The two had barely spoken in over twenty years.

Her mother was smoothing her skirt again. "Well, sweetheart, I've been doing some thinking. And I've come to the brilliant deduction that things change. If we want to survive in life, we have to adapt." Ingrid looked up. A rueful gleam lit those sea-blue eyes. "With Elli married and living in Gullandria, and with Brit suddenly deciding to—oh, how should I put it?—explore her Gullandrian roots—I can see I'll have to be willing to talk to Osrik now and then if I want to have any idea of what's going on in my daughters' lives."

"You could try asking us."

Ingrid made a sound of frustration low in her throat. "I have. I don't get a lot of answers—and what are you saying? That you'd rather your father and I went back to not speaking?"

Maybe she would. Especially if they were going

to discuss things like her sex life. "Whether you speak to him or not is completely up to you."

"Thank you, darling." There was a definite note of sarcasm.

Liv decided to ignore it. "So Father called and he told you..."

"About how you spent Midsummer's Eve, about how you experienced the Freyasdahl symptoms the following night, about Finn's offer of marriage and your refusal. Your father said Finn had decided to come here, to Sacramento, for a few weeks, to see if he might somehow manage to change your mind."

Liv felt her anger rising again. "And you want that to happen, right? You want him to change my mind. That's why you invited him to stay here, in the house where I grew up—to show your support for him. You actually think that I ought to marry him."

Ingrid reached out. "Oh, Livvy..."

Liv stepped back and sat in the chair across from her mother. "Just say it. You think I ought to marry him—marry a man I hardly know, a man with whom I have absolutely nothing in common, a man who's been under just about every skirt in Gullandria."

Ingrid said nothing. For a moment, they sat in silence, mother and daughter, at odds.

Then Ingrid was leaning forward again, a wild, warm light in her eyes. "Oh, Livvy. I *like* him. I do. And he's from a good family. And if you give it a chance, you might find the two of you have more in common than you realize. And besides, I saw the way he looked at you just now."

"Mom." Liv leaned forward, too. She spoke

softly, taking care that no one but Ingrid would hear. "He's a…playboy. Flirting to him is like breathing. He does it without having to give it a thought. He looks at *all* the women as if they're the only one."

"No, he does not. I'd bet a huge sum of money on that," said Ingrid firmly. "And please don't scowl. I do understand exactly what you mean when you speak of his flirting skills. He's flirted with *me,* for heaven's sake, and I loved it."

"Well, at least you admit it."

"Why shouldn't I? He's a joy to flirt with. But the way he looked at you…it was an altogether different thing."

Absurd, but Liv felt her heart lift a fraction. "Oh, I don't think so."

"You're so bright, Liv. So strong and sure. Focused and determined, way beyond your years. And you're also domineering. And overbearing. And it wouldn't hurt you to stop and smell the flowers now and then."

Liv tried to keep from rolling her eyes. "Your point being?"

"That I think Finn sees your value, as a person, as a woman he could love. And you have to admit—" her mother dared a naughty grin "—he's certainly experienced enough with the fairer sex to know a special woman when he meets her."

Liv did roll her eyes then. "That's an interesting way of looking at it."

"It's merely the truth."

"Mom. You are working on me."

"Yes, I am. I want you to give Finn a chance."

"I have a *boyfriend,* remember?"

''Darling. Simon Graves is a lovely man. But if he was really all that important to you, I doubt you would have spent Midsummer's Eve with Finn.''

Liv felt her face flaming. Okay, okay, maybe some of her fury at Finn was misdirected anger at herself. What she'd done with him four nights ago told her things about herself she really didn't need to know.

''Finn,'' Ingrid said, ''is, after all, the father of your child.''

Liv groaned. ''Please. It was only one night—to my lasting shame. And it's way too soon to—''

''No, it's not. What happened to you always happens to the Freyasdahl women when—''

''Mom. Let's just...not go there, okay? I've been over it with Brit and Father and Finn. I really don't feel up to going around and around about it with you, too.''

Her mother's eyes were very bright. ''There *will* be a baby. Deny it now, if you feel you have to. But that won't make it go away. And yes, I am... supporting Finn in this, in his effort to get to know you better. In his willingness to try and do the right thing. He seems a lovely man to me and he's welcome in my home. I'm only too happy that the father of your baby was well-brought-up, is well-to-do and wants to marry you and give your baby his name.''

''Oh, Mom...'' Liv knew she was softening. How could she help it, seeing the way her mother looked right now, that gleam in her eyes, the glow on her cheeks?

Liv supposed her mother's reaction wasn't surprising. A new baby in the family, to Ingrid, would mean new hope for the future, someone on whom to lavish all the love she'd never be able to give her lost sons.

"Darling, I'm not saying you should marry him just because of the baby. This is not Gullandria and you know your family will support you, whatever steps you feel you have to take. I'm only saying, what can it hurt to give Finn a chance?"

At dinner, by tacit agreement, they kept things light.

Finn entertained them with stories of his adventures during his first day in Sacramento. Yes, he confessed, he had once or twice driven over the speed limit.

"But, as luck would have it, no one was hurt."

He'd eaten lunch at McDonald's. "Excellent French fries." And pumped his own gas at a Jiffy ServeMart. "There was a small market beyond the pumps. I went inside. Rows of muffins and biscuits, individually packed. Racks and racks of crispy snacks made of mysterious ingredients the names of which I found difficult to pronounce. And self-serve beverages. They offered something called a Super Huge Gulp. A massive plastic cup and you fill it up yourself. In my rental car, along with the computerized mapping system and the state-of-the-art stereo, there's a small device between the seats for holding beverage cups. Not big enough to hold a Super Huge Gulp, however. I was forced to drink the entire thing before I dared to get back behind the wheel."

Ingrid suggested teasingly, "And from this you learned?"

He laughed. "Absolutely nothing." He asked Ingrid about her work. Liv's mother owned an antique shop in Old Sacramento. He listened, rapt, as she described how she'd sold two French Empire armchairs with bronze sphinx mounts and a Winged Victory gilt candelabra.

And then he turned to Liv. "And how are things at the Attorney General's Office? Did they manage to get along without you for an entire week?"

Liv admitted with a good-natured smile that somehow they had.

There were candles on the table, tall white tapers in her mother's favorite silver candlesticks. Liv looked across at Finn. His eyes met hers, gleaming more golden than amber with the candle flames reflected in them. She thought of the two of them, on Midsummer's Eve, dancing like moonstruck fools around that blazing Viking ship, the rim of the red Gullandrian midnight sun dropping at last below the horizon. Her pulse quickened. Her whole body was too warm.

She felt a smile quiver across her mouth as she accepted the fact that he was here, in Sacramento, that he really did seem to want to make it work between them. And even if she didn't believe it *could* work, even if she didn't really believe she was pregnant, even if the last thing she needed in her life, at her age, with her career goals, was a baby...

Well, if by some crazy trick of fate it turned out she *was* pregnant, her choice would have to be to keep the child. She had plenty of money, a loving family to provide emotional support and she was strong and self-directed. For her, it would be a coward's act to do otherwise. Yes, it would slow her down a little, as far as her goals were concerned. But it wouldn't stop her. *Nothing* would stop her. She meant to make a difference in the world, no matter what curves life decided throw her.

So all right. She would…work with Finn on this, on getting to know him better. After all, if it did turn out she was pregnant, whether they married in the end or not, she would still have to find a way to get along with her baby's father.

"Good night, darling. Drive carefully," Ingrid said, presenting her cheek for a kiss. "Finn will walk you to your car."

Liv hardly needed an escort out to the back driveway, but she didn't argue with her mother's obvious attempt to throw her and Finn together.

Side by side, she and the prince walked down the back steps and over to her waiting car. Liv found herself all too conscious of the way his arm twice, and oh-so-lightly, brushed hers.

The thick branches of an old oak had swallowed the light intended to brighten the area between the porte cochere and the garages. When they reached her car, they were in deep shadow.

She stopped before crossing around to the driver's side and leaned back against the passenger door.

Finn, as if invited, moved in close. "Do I detect a certain…softening in your attitude toward me?"

"Yes," she confessed, "I suppose you do. You and my father and my mother have worn me down. I *still* don't think I'm pregnant, but I'm willing to accept that it's a possibility. I'm willing to do what you suggested back in Gullandria, to spend the next few weeks getting to know you better, just in case we end up discovering that there's a baby on the way, after all.''

"Clearly a fate worse than death.'' He said the words lightly, but there was a note of rebuke in them, too.

She shrugged. "Well, I have to tell you, a baby was just not on my to-do list for at least another decade or so.''

"Sometimes,'' he whispered, "life refuses to go according to plan.''

They were quiet for a moment. From the corner of the yard, a cricket chirped steadily. And a block or so away, some lonely dog let out a long, sad howl. The night was clear. And warm. The white disc of a full moon rode high in the sky, partly obscured, from where they stood, by the branches of the oak overhead.

As the dog's forlorn howl faded to nothing, Finn laughed. The sound was low and achingly sensual. "I have an idea.''

She looked at him warily. "Oh, no.''

He put a hand to either side of her, resting his palms on the car behind her, trapping her gently between his outstretched arms. "Let me come with you to that house on T Street.'' He smelled of lovely, tempting things. A hint of heather, a suggestion of musk...

"How do you know I'm staying on T Street?''

"I asked your mother. She told me everything I needed to know—address, house phone, cellular phone. I have it all. I can call you or find you at my will.''

''You know no shame.''

''So I've been told.''

''And I have to ask…''

''Anything.''

''Don't you have any responsibilities in Gullandria? Can you really afford to just take off out of nowhere and stay on for weeks in another country?''

''Liv darling, you've got your Puritan face on—your eyes narrowed, your nose scrunched up, that beautiful mouth of yours pinched up tight.''

She stuck out her chin at him, scrunched her nose harder and pinched her mouth up all the tighter.

''Gruesome,'' he said, and they laughed together. Then he explained, ''I have estate managers. I pay them. They manage. And should there be a terrible crisis of some sort, they know how to reach me. I also expend a considerable amount of effort—much more than I would ever admit to any casual acquaintance—managing a hefty stock portfolio. For that, in the past few years, all I need is a computer with an Internet connection and a telephone or two. Your mother has been so gracious as to give me one of the upstairs rooms to use as an office during my stay in America.''

''You're admitting then, that you actually do work.''

''Please don't tell anyone.''

''My lips are sealed.''

''Ah. Your lips…'' He leaned a fraction closer.

She brought a hand up, palm out, between his mouth and hers. He made a low, impatient noise in his throat. But he did back off. And she asked, "What about family? I seem to remember, at some point during the time we spent together in Gullandria, you mentioned a sister and a grandfather?"

"Yes." He shook his head. "My sister, Eveline, is sixteen. She lives at Balmarran. She's utterly unmanageable, I'm afraid. She drives tutors and companions away effortlessly, usually on the day my grandfather hires them. And then there was the recent upheaval over the groundskeeper's boy. The two decided they were in love. The boy is totally unsuitable for her, of course."

Egalitarian to the core, Liv put on her most socially superior expression. "Because he's a mere freeman?"

"Not really. I think my grandfather and I are enlightened enough to accept that my sister might someday decide to marry a man without a title."

"Then why?"

"You'd have to meet the boy. Cauley is completely uncivilized. He was ten when the groundskeeper and his wife adopted him. It was probably a mistake that they took him on. He was angry and aggressive, couldn't read or even write his own name. He's seventeen now. Under all the hair and the surly attitude, I'd venture to say he's a handsome young man, if a trifle too thin. But he remains woefully undereducated and socially inept. He's good in the gardens, though. His father has him working with his top assistant, Dag, learning the ropes, as they say."

"And he and your sister?"

"She seems, I'm somewhat relieved to say, to have tired of him."

"Only somewhat relieved?"

Finn shrugged. "I can't help but pity Cauley. He's hopelessly in love with her still. She's hurt him terribly and he's pulled into his shell even deeper than before."

"Back to your sister."

"If you insist."

"How has she been allowed to become so unmanageable?"

"My mother died when she was born, and my father soon after, of a broken heart. My grandfather is her guardian. He's never been able to refuse her anything."

There was, she realized, so very much she didn't know. "Your grandfather, what's his name?"

"Balder."

"A true Norse name."

He laughed. "How would you know?"

"My mother taught us the myths—at least the major ones. Balder, as I recall, was the son of Odin and Filgg. He was much beloved by the gods. His mother fixed it so nothing could kill him."

"Except a dart made of mistletoe." He leaned in closer again. "Take me home with you...."

She breathed in the intoxicating scent of him, admired the shadowed shape of his mouth, felt the pull of his gaze through the darkness. His suggestion did tempt her—far too much. "Uh-uh."

He bent closer. "Allow me the opportunity to convince you...." His mouth was an inch from hers. So far, she'd resisted the desire to kiss him. But she was weakening. And with his mouth so close, she couldn't keep herself from thinking that if she were to move toward him a fraction, their lips would meet.

"I don't..." She hadn't the faintest idea what she'd meant to say next.

"Like this." He leaned forward the necessary minute distance. His mouth touched hers—too briefly. And then he pulled back. "What would you like, Liv?"

"I..."

"What do you want?" As if he didn't know very well. "A kiss?"

How was she supposed to make a rational decision, with his arms on either side of her and his wonderful, hard body brushing the front of her and his lips no more than a breath away?

No doubt about it. It was happening again, that distressing problem he so easily created whenever he was near: the problem of a precipitous drop in her IQ....

And just look what he had done, after tempting her so thoroughly? He'd ended by making it, undeniably, her choice.

She wasn't as strong as she probably should have been, as strong as she'd always considered herself until recently—recently being ever since she'd met this particular impossible, too-charming man. "Oh, Finn." And then she was leaning into him, capturing that wonderful, skilled, hot mouth of his.

He took care of the rest. Those lean arms closed around her and his body pressed close. And his mouth....

With a small, lost cry of surrender, Liv wrapped her arms around his neck.

His tongue entered quickly, sliding along the top of hers, pushing all the way in, then slowly, teasingly retreating.

No way could she stop her own tongue from following, into the hot, wet cave beyond his lips. His teeth closed, lightly, and her tongue was captive. And then there was his tongue again, slipping beneath hers in a liquid, oh-so-lovely caress.

Oh, how did he do it? When Finn Danelaw kissed her, she went spinning, deliciously, out of control. His hands moved, pressing, rubbing, down over the curve of her bottom, and back up, insinuating themselves under the hem of her gauzy blouse, so he could rub and stroke her up and down her spine. Her skin burned and tingled everywhere that he touched. His mouth held hers captive as his tongue worked its hot magic. One hand curved possessively at her waist while the other was slipping around to the front of her, then moving, oh-so-slowly down....

And down...

And if they kept on like this, they'd end up stretched out naked on her mother's driveway.

Uh-uh.

From some source of good sense she'd almost forgotten she possessed, she slid her palms down to his chest and exerted a light but definite pressure.

After a moment, with obvious reluctance, he lifted his head. She saw the white flash of his teeth in the darkness. "Change your mind?"

What mind? "About?"

"Allowing me to come home with you."

She sucked in a calming breath, let it out very carefully and shook her head.

He looked at her for a long moment. Finally he asked with rueful good humor, "That wasn't a no, was it?"

"It was."

"How discouraging."

"But tomorrow night—"

His teeth flashed again. "At last."

"You didn't let me finish." Her lips felt swollen, tender. Hot. She had to resist the urge to raise a hand and touch them. "I was going to say we'd go to dinner, if you'd like."

"Dinner." It clearly was not what he'd had in mind.

"Yes, dinner. We'll talk. We'll...enjoy each other's company."

"I'm all for enjoyment, in any form."

"It's a date, then—say seven-thirty, my house?"

"I'll be there."

She felt his heart beating under her hand. And it was crazy, but she could have stood there forever, with Finn, in her mother's driveway, surrounded by warm summer darkness, beneath the old oak tree. "I...well, I guess there are things to be said for relentless pursuit."

He caught one of her hands and kissed the tops of her knuckles, causing them to tingle in a heady, lovely way. "I assure you, my darling, I have only begun to assail the walls around your stubborn heart."

Chapter Eight

Liv's cell phone rang as she was pulling in beneath the carport at the back of her borrowed house on T Street. She dug the thing out of her purse and flipped it open.

The number in the display was to Simon's cell.

For a moment of which she was not the least bit proud, she considered not answering. Then, thoroughly disgusted with herself, she pushed the talk button and put the phone to her ear.

"Liv?"

"Hi."

"At last, I caught you." He sounded...she couldn't tell. Worried? Suspicious? Maybe he had read about her and Finn in the tabloids.

"Liv? Are you there?"

"Right here. And it's been pretty crazy, since I

got back. I should have called you, I know, but I..."
She what? There was no excuse for not having called
him. She finished lamely, "Well, it's been such a
zoo...."

"Where are you now?"

"I just got home—to the T Street house?" She
pressed her fingers to her lips. It seemed as if she
could still feel the hot pressure of Finn's mouth there.
Fifteen minutes ago, in her mother's driveway, with
Finn's arms around her, she'd felt pretty good about
everything. She was finally taking charge, dealing
with the mess she'd made in a way that everyone
involved—meaning herself and her family and Finn
and the baby that might or might not be coming—
could accept.

Simon hadn't figured in the equation. She hadn't
so much as considered him. Which made her feel like
something very low—a snail, a slug—something that
crawls along the ground and leaves a slime trail.

"Liv, are you all right?"

"Fine. Really. And where has the future senator
dragged you off to this week?"

"Right here," he said, and again named the hotel
he'd mentioned in his phone message yesterday.
"Remember, the rally today?"

"Oh. Yes. The rally. Of course." The one she'd
promised to attend. "I'm sorry, Simon. As I said, it's
just been—"

"Never mind," he said glumly. "It's okay."

They both knew it wasn't. She asked, too brightly,
"How did it go?"

"Great."

"Well. Hey. Okay."

"We're leaving for Salinas tomorrow. He's got a speech Wednesday, the UFW branch there. I was hoping, maybe, I could see you tonight."

"Ah," she said, as if that were an answer.

He asked nervously, "Where have you been, anyway?"

"Dinner. At Mom's." It was the truth, just not *all* of it. Oh, she despised herself more by the minute.

"Well," he said, all glumness again. "It *is* late. I'm sure you're tired."

No more excuses, she lectured herself. She had to stop putting this off. "Why don't you come over."

"Right now?"

"Yes."

"Good," he said, suddenly firm. "I think I should. I think we need to talk."

Simon appeared at the door ten minutes later. Liv saw the paper rolled in his fist and knew he'd been reading about her supposed engagement to Finn.

"*The World Tattler,*" he said, and tried to smile. "Hot off the presses."

The World Tattler was jam-packed with photos of her and Finn at the airport yesterday. The story included the obligatory rehash of the old, sad tale of how her mother, an American heiress of Gullandrian descent, had traveled to the land of her forefathers and met Osrik Thorson, the soon-to-be king. After a whirlwind fairy-tale courtship, they'd wed; she'd borne him five children—two sons and triplet daughters—and then left him, taking the three tiny princesses to raise as Americans. The deaths of Liv's brothers received mention under the heading, Tragedy Upon Tragedy. And then there was the bit about Elli and Hauk: The Princess And Her Warrior Groom.

And last but not least, the intrepid *Tattler* staff had managed to dig up a few pictures of Finn escorting past girlfriends. The caption read, Former Flames Of The Playboy Prince. Liv couldn't help noting that the women were all gorgeous, much better looking than she. One was a fairly well known Danish actress with absolutely spectacular breasts. All the women seemed to glow from within, as if they'd found true love at last.

"Charming," Liv said with a scowl.

"Liv, what is going on?" Simon looked at her as if she'd stabbed him to the heart. "Are you marrying this guy?"

"No."

"But—"

"Simon."

"Yes?" He looked at her desperately, longing for her to explain.

There was nothing to explain. In fact, there was only one thing to say. "I'm sorry, Simon. I've behaved badly. Things are...suddenly all turned around in my life. I asked you here to tell you I won't be seeing you anymore."

"You mean you're in love with this guy?"

"No." She said it far too quickly, as if she had to deny it to herself, which was crazy. Of course, she wasn't in love with Finn. She was...kind of nuts about him, okay. A little bit out of her head when he was around. It was purely physical, and she was ashamed to admit her own—oh, what to call it—her purely sexual weakness? But as to her heart? It wasn't involved.

Simon was still sitting there, waiting for her to make it all clear to him. She tried again. "I mean...oh, Simon. You and I, well, we never had any real commitment. We just shared a sort of unspoken understanding. And I've realized in the last few days that I can't, um, share that with you anymore."

Simon was crushed.

He swore, whatever she'd done, it didn't matter. He didn't *own* her—but they were so *close*. They had so much they shared. They'd both dedicated their lives to working for positive political change. She couldn't really be thinking about marrying the playboy prince, could she? Wouldn't she please reconsider? He didn't want to *lose* her....

Liv only kept repeating, "Oh, Simon. I'm so sorry, Simon. But I can't see you anymore...."

Finally he said goodbye, looking dazed and beaten, leaving her feeling as if she'd just spent forty-five minutes or so torturing a small, defenseless animal.

The next day, guilt over what she'd done to poor Simon, and a worrisome combination of dread and anticipation at the thought of seeing Finn again that evening, made it hard to concentrate on filing and word processing and on the law books opened in front of her with their endless columns of tiny print. The attorney general himself came by her desk and asked her a question. She jumped and blinked and said, "Huh?" like some idiot with no background, who had no idea at all of how to handle herself.

Her life was in shambles. She'd broken poor Simon's honest, steadfast heart. She might or might not be having the baby of a man who'd made love with hundreds of gorgeous, willing, large-breasted women. Her mother *and* her father *and* her sister all believed there was a baby coming. And her mother and her father thought she ought to marry the seductive stranger who'd supposedly impregnated her.

And whenever she wasn't thinking about the abject awfulness of her situation, she would find herself wandering off into misty, lustful daydreams in which she did with Finn the very things that had gotten her into this predicament in the first place.

Strangely, her memories of Midsummer's Eve, the ones she'd thought lost in a haze of too much ale, seemed to be slowly coming back to her. She remembered lying naked in the clearing, both of them on their sides, her leg slung over his lean hip. He was inside her, but they weren't moving.

Well, except for their hands and their mouths. They lay there, joined, and kissed and kissed and kissed some more. She combed his silky hair with her fingers, and he stroked her—long, slow caresses, his hand sliding over her shoulder, down her arm, into the curve of her waist, up over the cocked slope of her lifted hip, along her thigh....

His finger trailed inward, following the shadowed place where her thigh met the cradle of her hips, now and then pausing to pet the dark blond curls there. And then, as she started moaning low in her throat, he'd touched her cleft, his finger trailing in, finding the center of her pleasure within the slick folds and—

"Liv, are you sick?" one of the clerks asked.

She blinked and sat up straight and announced, "Oh, no. Just fine. Just terrific. Really."

"Just wondered. You look kind of dazed, you know? Staring into space with your mouth hanging open."

At the water cooler, two of the secretaries who'd been whispering gleefully to each other fell instantly silent when she approached. And she found a copy of *The World Tattler* in the break room.

It was absolutely awful. She thought that day would never end. She was never in her life so grateful to see five o'clock come around.

The bell rang right at seven. She marched down the stairs and yanked open the door.

In a soft short-sleeved gray silk shirt and black slacks, Finn stood there looking ready for anything. Oh, come on now, did any man have a right to be so sexy?

"Well," she said sourly, "if it isn't the Playboy Prince."

He made a tsking sound. "Don't tell me. You've been reading *The World Tattler*. Darling Liv, I know you've got better things to do with your time."

"I had," she announced, "a very bad day." He stepped forward. She stepped back. He reached behind him, caught the door and pushed it shut. "Why don't you come on in?" she scoffed.

"Thanks, I will." He looked around the old-fashioned foyer with its cabbage-rose wallpaper and mahogany wainscoting. "Charming little place." And then he looked right at her. "You'll get wrinkles, scowling all the time like that."

"My life is just not turning out the way I planned." She knew she sounded petulant and spoiled, and right at that moment, she didn't even care.

She looked down. He'd done it again. Without her even realizing it was happening, his hand was wrapped around hers. It felt very good—warm and strong. Reassuring. Encompassing.

She glared up at him. "Did I give you my hand?"

His mouth curved lazily. "I took it."

She knew she should yank it away or demand he give it back. But what good would that do? He'd only capture it again. He'd keep capturing it and capturing it until she finally gave in and let him have it.

Might as well just cut to the chase and let him have it now.

He said, "You need a drink."

"I'll never drink again, and besides, what if I *am* pregnant? It wouldn't be good for the baby."

"Ah. You may be right. But do you have whiskey?"

"Yeah. On the sideboard in the dining room."

"May I have some?"

She grumbled her answer. "Oh, I suppose."

"Which way?"

"Let go of my hand and I'll show you."

"Never. Lead the way."

So she took him through the sitting room into the dining room and showed him the crystal carafe half-full of amber liquid. He poured two finger's worth into a short glass with his free hand.

"Your dexterity amazes me," she remarked as he sipped.

"Yes. It's true I have always been...good with my hands." He tipped his glass at her. "To my favorite princess." He sipped again, then raised her hand and pressed his lips to the back of it, causing the usual heated thrill to shimmer through her. "Come. Let's sit down for a moment." He pulled her to the settee in the sitting room, sat and dragged her down beside him. "Now." He released her hand and sat back. "Tell me all."

"All?"

"Your terrible day. What is it that has you growling and scowling?"

"You don't want to know."

"Liv darling, trust me. If I don't want to know, I won't ask."

She muttered, "They're whispering about me at the water cooler."

"This water cooler, I take it, is in the Attorney General's Office where you work?"

"Exactly."

"Ah. And you've never been whispered about before?"

"Oh, of course I have. But only by extension."

He frowned. "By extension?"

"Well, I mean, because I'm a princess. Because my mother is the Runaway Gullandrian Queen. All that old garbage. Never before because of..." She didn't know quite how to put it.

He did. "Something you did yourself?"

"But I *didn't*."

He only looked at her.

"Okay, I did do...something I shouldn't have. But nobody knows about that—I mean, outside of you and my father and Prince Medwyn.'' He was looking at her sideways. She made an impatient sound in her throat. ''All right. And my mother and my sister and a nosy Gullandrian maid—oh, and don't look at me like that. You're right, I know. Since *that* many people know, it wouldn't be surprising if there were others. But what we did on Midsummer's Eve didn't make the tabloids. Our supposed engagement did. I know my father planted that story, that he had all those reporters waiting for us at the airport Sunday night. I hate reading lies about myself, and knowing my father perpetrated those lies makes it all the worse.''

Finn set his empty glass on the coffee table in front of them. Then he looked at her again, an odd sort of look this time, one that made her wonder what he might be up to. Finally he asked, ''Why would he do that? What would it get him?''

''I don't know. Maybe he did it for spite.''

''I have served your father most of my life. His Majesty does nothing for spite. He will go far, it's true, to get what he wants. He's made it very clear he wants you to marry me. The question is, how would his lying about it to the press help him accomplish that goal? As far as I can see, it only made you more angry and unwilling, created more barriers for me to break down.''

''He didn't know that when he leaked the story.''

''Liv. He's not a fool. He's spent enough time with you to see you're not a woman to roll over and play dead when you're crossed.''

Liv thought about that one for a moment, then admitted, ''All right. You may have a point.''

''What's that I hear? An actual concession?''

''Don't expect a lot of them—and maybe he did it to…scare someone away.''

Finn rose, carried his glass to the sideboard and poured another drink. He didn't speak until he'd returned to the sitting area and taken the space beside her again. ''Someone like…?''

She thought of poor Simon, looking at her with those big, lost puppy-dog eyes. Oh, why was she telling Finn this? It didn't seem right, somehow.

''Liv,'' he said softly. ''Tell me. Now.'' Beneath the velvet of his voice, there lay a hint of steel.

''You have no right to—''

''Tell me.'' He had her hand again. His grip was gentle, but she knew if she tried to shake him off, she wouldn't succeed. There was, she kept discovering, more to the playboy prince than met the eye.

''Simon.'' She said the name grudgingly. ''Simon Graves. I think I mentioned him to you before, didn't I? He's a law student at Stanford. Third year. We've been…together, for about eighteen months.''

''And you think your father…''

''Maybe he wanted Simon out of the picture. Maybe he thought a big tabloid spread about you, me and wedding bells would do it.''

''Well, did it work? Is Simon 'out of the picture'?''

She saw what was going on, then. ''It was *you*, wasn't it? You planted the story.''

He gave her the laziest one-shoulder shrug. ''Well, yes. I did.''

''To get Simon 'out of the picture.' ''

''Guilty as charged—and did it work?''

She realized she wasn't as angry as she probably should have been. Breaking it off with Simon was something she *had* needed to do. Finn's lie to the tabloids had only forced her to do it sooner rather than later.

"Yes," she confessed, "it worked."

He waited, looking at her steadily.

"What?" she demanded.

"Tell me more."

"Such as?"

He shrugged again—a lift and drop of that one shoulder. It seemed, on the surface, a casual movement. "Was Simon Graves your lover?"

She didn't answer.

"Do you love him?"

"Of course, I love him." She said it automatically. With a total lack of ardor that told volumes more than she'd intended to reveal.

Finn didn't move, but a certain edge of coiled intensity seemed to drain from him. "Ah. *That* kind of love."

She jerked her hand free. "I care for Simon. A lot."

"And was he your lover?"

"Didn't I just *not* answer that question a minute ago?"

"Was he?"

Liv wanted to grab his drink from where he'd set it on the table and toss it in his face. She restrained herself and spoke with measured care. "Why don't we talk about a few of your old girlfriends? That Danish actress, for instance, the one whose picture they ran in the *Tattler?* Or the lady I saw you dancing with that first night at my father's court? Or…any woman. Pick a woman. I know there have been plenty.''

Finn didn't answer immediately. They enjoyed a mini stare-down. Finally he nodded. ''Point taken.''

She relaxed a little. ''Well, okay.''

After a moment he volunteered levelly, ''There's no one now. No one but you.''

Ha. ''Since Sunday, anyway.''

He grinned. ''That's right.''

And maybe, she decided, Finn did deserve to hear a few specifics about what had happened last night between her and Simon. She volunteered, only a little bit reluctantly, ''As far as Simon and me, he came to see me last night. He'd read the *Tattler* article. He was upset. I told him that I wouldn't be seeing him anymore. And I sent him away.''

Something flared in Finn's incredible eyes. ''You do believe you're pregnant, then.''

''No, I don't. My symptoms the other night could far too easily be nothing more than a psychosomatic reaction based on a family superstition.''

''A psychosomatic reaction that you experienced because…?''

''I was absolutely disgusted with myself.''

''For making love with me, you mean?''

She winced.

Finn laughed. ''I think I heard somewhere that you plan to go into politics.''

She admitted ruefully, ''Okay, okay. I need to work on my diplomacy a little.''

''It's a thought—and back to Simon.''

''Do we have to?''

"Yes. If you don't believe you're pregnant, then why did you break it off with him?"

"Because you're right about one thing. What I felt for Simon was *that* kind of love. And what I did with you the other night has made me see that Simon really isn't the man for me any more than I'm the woman for him."

There was a long, quite beautiful moment. He regarded her steadily. She didn't look away.

Then he took his glass from the table and raised it in her direction once more. "Well said."

Liv nodded graciously.

Finn drank. "Another question."

"Why stop now?"

"Given that you don't believe you're pregnant, why am I here, in your sitting room?"

"Because I'm willing to admit I *might* be pregnant. And if I am, I realize I *will* have to deal with you."

"You certainly will."

"Don't be overbearing. I said that I would."

"I seek clarity only, my love."

"Right. And since when did I become your love?"

"Since the moment I first saw you."

"If you think I believe that, maybe you have a bridge you can sell me."

He frowned for a moment, then his fine brow smoothed out. "Ah. One of your clever Americanisms." He brought the hand he was forever capturing to his mouth. Her skin tingled deliciously at the touch of his lips. "You could marry me now...."

"I could climb Mount Everest. Go skydiving. Jump off the Empire State Building."

"Meaning?"

She pulled her hand free for about the hundredth time. "Just because I *can* do something doesn't mean I will."

They walked to a restaurant not far from the house, shared a leisurely meal, then strolled back together.

They'd taken perhaps ten steps along the sidewalk when Finn's hand closed over hers. Liv didn't remark on it or try to pull away.

By then, it was a little after nine and night had fallen. The streetlamps made warm pools of light on the sidewalks and the sycamores and maples rustled softly in a gentle breeze. The Sacramento summer, so far, had been a mild one. The nights, as yet, were balmy. Perfect for an evening stroll.

They went up the wide stone steps to the inviting wooden porch where a swing, suspended from the eaves, swayed slightly, as if an invisible occupant had just jumped up to greet them.

They sat down and swung idly back and forth.

"A porch swing is so American," Finn said. "Always, in your American movies, the young lovers sit out in them, on nights like this." He raised his left arm and laid it along the back of the swing, behind her. "Casually, the young quarterback puts his arm in position."

She sent him a look. "Quarterback?"

"Always, in your American movies, the young lover is a quarterback. He scores the winning touchdown for the home team. And then later, he sits out on the front porch in the swing with his girl—a front porch very much like this one, a swing no different

than the one we're sitting in now. And he prepares
to score in another deeper, more intimate way.''

''Which movie, specifically, are we talking about
here?''

''Wait.'' He put up his right hand. ''Look over
there.'' He pointed toward the rosebush twining over
the thick stone porch rail. She strained to see, and
his other arm settled across her shoulder.

She turned to him again. ''Smooth.''

He pulled her closer. ''I'll wager you know what
comes next.''

She breathed in the scent of him. So tempting.

Oh, what could be the harm in a kiss?

Or two.

She whispered, ''Show me.'' The swing moved
gently back and forth, back and forth. Liv tipped her
head up, offering her mouth.

He wasted no time in taking it.

They sat on that swing for over an hour, swaying
and kissing, whispering together. He said he'd never
gone to a school until he was a young man and attended University at Oslo. ''I lived at Balmarran.
There were tutors, excellent ones.''

''How old were you, when your mother died?''

''Twelve.''

''And thirteen, when you lost your father?''

He made a noise in the affirmative.

''Tough times, huh?''

''Don't forget. I had my baby sister to keep me
company. Wretched child. She cried for two years
without stopping, or at least, it seemed that way to
me.''

''You adore her.''

"I never said that."

"You didn't have to. I can tell by your voice when you talk about her."

"My grandfather is still strong and healthy at seventy-eight. But Eveline will drive him to his grave. Of late, since her attraction to the groundskeeper's boy began to pall, she speaks of running off to the wilds beyond the Black Mountains, to become a *kvina soldar.*"

"*Kvina soldar?* Woman warrior, right?"

"Very good. I'll make a Gullandrian of you yet."

"Never. I'm American to the core."

"We'll see about that."

"I can hardly be governor of California if I'm living in Gullandria."

"Ah. You're willing to discuss where we're going to live."

"What's to discuss? I'll live here. You'll live there."

"Hardly my idea of a marriage."

"But Finn, I'm not going to—"

"Shh." He laid a finger against her mouth. And then that finger lightly brushed over her cheek and into her hair. He cupped the back of her head, brought his lips so close to hers...

How could she resist? She gave him her mouth and he gave her another of those lovely, deep, wet, lingering kisses. The swing softly swayed. The crickets sang in the grass.

Sometime later, she rested her head on his shoulder and whispered, "When my sisters and I were little, on nights like this, we'd take our sleeping bags out to the backyard, roll them out on the grass and spend the night under the stars. We'd pick out the constellations and tell each other scary stories. Even at the age of seven or eight, Brit could tell a scary story with the best of them. More than once, she had me so terrified I would have given just about anything to wiggle out of my sleeping bag and run for the safety of the house.''

He nuzzled a kiss into her hair. ''But of course, you couldn't.''

She pulled back a fraction so she could look at him. ''How did you know that?''

''You would want no one—not even your sisters—to see your fear. They might think you weak. You despise weakness in yourself, though I'd guess you would be willing to tolerate it, to an extent anyway, in those that you love.''

He had it exactly right. She smiled at him through the darkness. Then, with a sigh, she rested her head on his shoulder once more.

''I have to go in,'' she said a long time later.

He caught her chin, guided it up and brushed another kiss across her mouth. ''I'll come in with you....''

''It's tempting. Very tempting.''

''So why resist?''

A few hours ago, she would have had an instant answer to that one. Now she was finding herself perilously close to agreeing with him.

They were both adults, both—since she had said goodbye to poor Simon—unencumbered by other commitments. And they wouldn't be doing anything they hadn't done before.

But she whispered, ''No,'' anyway. Tenderly. With regret.

* * *

The next day, as Finn sat in the office room at Ingrid's house, checking his stocks and speaking with a London broker he often used, the other line blinked red.

He looked at the display and recognized the number. "I'll ring you back," he said to the broker. He punched the second line. "Your Majesty. I am honored."

"How goes it?"

Finn sat back in his chair and stared, unseeing, at the columns of figures on his computer screen. He thought of the night before, of all the lingering, maddening kisses. Of how, in the end, Liv had sent him away. "She's an amazing woman, your daughter."

The king grunted. "She has yet to say yes."

"That's correct."

"*The World Tattler* says otherwise."

Finn chuckled. "Sadly, the *Tattler*'s sources are often untrustworthy."

"*My* sources tell me my daughter is…softening."

"Softening." Finn pondered the word. "Yes, sire. I think I can safely claim that to be so."

"We have reason then, to be optimistic?"

"Yes, Your Majesty. I believe we do…."

Chapter Nine

That evening Liv and Finn went to the movies. The night after that, they ordered in. Friday, they went to a play in the park. And Saturday, they rode up into the foothills. Finn drove. He kept the music up way too loud. And he made jokes about that extra brake pedal she appeared to have on her side of the car.

Liv found Nevada City as charming as ever, with its adorable Victorians in close rows, the slopes of the hills blanketed in tall evergreen and the oaks and maples thick with their summer leaves. They wandered the steep streets of downtown, window-shopping, stopping to look inside when a particular store caught their fancy. Later they shared a picnic in Pioneer Park.

It was after dark when they got back to the T Street house. Finn came in for a couple of hours.

They watched a movie, a bowl of popcorn on the couch between them, losing track of the story as they kept bending across the bowl to enjoy an endless string of lovely, salty kisses. Somehow, though, she managed to send him away before bedtime.

It wasn't easy, keeping Finn out of her bed. He was so very skilled at tempting her to let him in. Liv spent more time than she would ever admit dreaming about doing with him what she kept insisting they weren't going to do. Mostly, she was able to confine her dreams to the appropriate situations: mornings, over a cup of herb tea; when she was in Finn's arms—and at night, after she sent him away.

Happily, fantasies of making love with Finn brought only pleasure now. They didn't torture her in daylight, or keep her awake too long at night. She was sleeping well and she was pulling her weight at work again, word processing with the best of them, answering phones with cheer and efficiency, ready and willing to "gofer" whatever needed getting.

On Monday, she saw the new issue of *The World Tattler* on the table in the break room. She couldn't resist thumbing through it.

She and Finn didn't rate their own article in that one. Just a couple of snapshots in a spread titled Young Royals In Love. There was a shot of them walking up Commercial Street in Nevada City, hand in hand, their heads turned toward each other, both of them grinning. And another of them sitting close together at the Land Park amphitheater, eyes forward, focused on the play.

It wasn't so bad, really. At least they'd only been caught during their more…public moments. She didn't find a single shot of them locked in a torrid embrace on her front porch swing or anything.

And besides, wasn't it something she'd have to get used to—reporters trailing her, asking questions, taking pictures? She planned, after all, a very public kind of life for herself.

"Lookin' good, there, Liv." It was one of the file clerks, peering over her shoulder.

Liv only smiled. "Hey, thanks, Orinda."

In his office room, Finn picked up the phone. "Your Majesty. I trust you are well."

"I didn't call to speak of my health. My sources tell me you're with my daughter constantly."

Finn turned in his swivel chair and looked out the window at a lush-leaved oak in his hostess's backyard. "Your sources have it right."

There was a silence. Then the king prompted, "Well?"

"My lord, progress is slower than I would wish."

"I'm told you always leave her house well before morning light."

"Your men are most impressively observant."

"Take her to bed. A woman is always more easily led after thorough pleasuring."

"Excellent advice, my lord."

"*Have* you taken her to bed as of yet?"

"Your Majesty, we wouldn't be in this predicament had I not."

"Don't toy with me, Finn."

"My liege, there are some things a man hesitates to discuss, even with his king."

Again the line was silent, except for the faint

crackle of static. Finally the king said, "Perhaps you have a point."

"Thank you, Your Majesty."

"I want to know immediately when she says yes."

"And you shall."

"And Finn?"

"Yes, Your Majesty?"

"Remember the words of Odin himself. 'The hearts of women were fashioned on a spinning wheel.' Those of the fairer sex are by nature capricious. Don't allow her forever to make up her mind. She will take eternity—and then demand another day."

"Marry me," Finn said that night. They were sitting in the porch swing. Swaying. Kissing.

"Oh, Finn."

He captured her chin. "Tell me that means yes."

She wrapped her hand around his wrist and held on. They stared at each other as the crickets sang and a siren started low in the distance, the sound swelling until it passed a few blocks away and then fading off into the summer night.

He asked, "When you know you're pregnant, will you marry me then?"

"I...don't know."

He let go. For a moment, she thought he was angry. And then, very slowly, he smiled. "A week ago, you would have said absolutely not."

He was right. But that didn't mean she could ever, realistically, say yes. She knew that the future she planned for herself could still be made to happen, even if she was pregnant and had her baby without benefit of marriage. Single motherhood, in America, was becoming, more and more, an acceptable way to raise children. In a decade or two, she felt certain, single mothers would be running for Congress.

But there was no way she'd ever realize her ambitions if she married Finn and moved to Gullandria.

She whispered, "One thing I do know…"

He grabbed her hand and laid it flat against his hard chest. "How do you say it? Hit me with it. Right here."

"Well, I just can't see…how it can work. No matter what happens, I'm not running off to live in your castle in Gullandria. I'm staying here. I'm finishing law school. I'm—"

He put his finger to her lips again, signaling for silence. "I think 'I don't know' is enough for tonight."

The next night, he showed up at her door with a home pregnancy test kit tucked under one arm, the instruction sheet open in his hands. "Look, my love. It says here, 'Ninety-nine percent effective one day after—'"

She took his arm, dragged him inside and firmly shut the door. "Where did you get that?"

"Albertson's Food and Drug, it was called. The pharmacy section. The clerks there were marvelously helpful."

"I'll bet." People—especially *female* people—fell all over themselves when Finn needed aid.

"You didn't let me finish. It says, 'Ninety-nine percent effective one day after a missed menstrual period.'"

"Oh, that's so lovely to know."

He sent her a fond smile. "And when would that be—for you?"

She wondered why she felt so resentful. It was a perfectly reasonable question, given the situation.

"Liv?"

"What?" It came out sounding much too hostile.

He folded up the instruction sheet and set it and the kit on the entry hall table. Then he turned back to her and waited, arms crossed over that broad chest, feet planted wide apart, as if taking a stand in a strong wind.

After a stubborn twenty seconds or so, she muttered, "I'd have to look at my calendar."

"And where is your calendar?"

She knew by the expression on his face that there was no way to get out of this gracefully. She also knew there was no real reason she should *want* to get out of it. Whether or not she was actually pregnant was the main question, after all.

Still she resisted. "You know, Finn, I think my biological functions should be my own business."

He regarded her from under slightly lowered brows. "Darling. Please get the calendar."

She had her own feet planted apart now, her arms folded over her middle, in a mirror of his pose. "I do resent this."

"You being you, I'm certain you do."

"What is *that* supposed to mean?"

"You're an intelligent woman. My guess is you already know."

They shared one of their stare-downs. A very long one. Out on T Street, a car went by, stereo booming out, heavy on the bases. As the hollow beat faded away, an ice-cream truck rolled slowly past, playing "It's a Small World, After All" in the usual tinkling organ-grinder style of ice-cream trucks everywhere.

In the end, Liv was the one who blinked. "I suppose you'll stand there forever, refusing to budge, until I get you what you want."

For that, she got the tiniest lift of one side of his beautiful mouth. And other than that, absolute stillness.

"Oh, all right," she muttered, then commanded, "wait here."

She pounded up the stairs and stomped down the hall to the bedroom that was hers for the duration of her stay in the house. The calendar hung on a suction hook over the small cherry-wood desk in the corner, by the mirrored mahogany wardrobe. She had a palm planner, but she used it for appointments and school and business. She liked a nice big old-fashioned wall calendar for personal stuff—birthdays and dates with the hairdresser and keeping track of her periods.

She snatched the calendar off the wall and turned to the previous month. She was pretty sure her last one had started a week before she left for Gullandria. It had been Friday, hadn't it? And she'd had to run to the ladies' room to take care of the problem.

However, it appeared she'd forgotten to mark it down on her calendar.

Well, well. Too bad.

She started to hang the thing back on the wall, but then she remembered that look in Finn's eyes. He was truly the most persistent man she'd ever had the inconvenience—and yes, all right, the pleasure—to get to know. Better to simply take it down to him and show him that whenever it had been, she'd failed to make a note of it.

Finn was waiting right there at the bottom when she descended with the calendar. He watched her come down to him, a gleam of pure suspicion in his eyes. "I'm not sure I like that smile. It's much too smug. Also, you've stopped pounding around like an elephant on the rampage. These are not good signs."

"An elephant, huh? That's not very flattering."

"Let me see it."

She reached the bottom and handed him the calendar. "Sorry. It appears that, whenever it was, I forgot to mark it down."

He studied the page for June, pointed to a small pen mark on Wednesday, the fifth. "What about this?"

"A smudge. I draw a star in the upper left hand corner of the box for the first day."

He looked at her probingly, then accused, "You do remember when it was, don't you?"

She didn't lie—exactly. "It was a hectic month. The end of school, finals, all that, followed by the move here and starting a new job. And then off to Gullandria and my, er, whirlwind week with you."

He flipped the page back to May. Pointed at the tiny star in the square for the eleventh. "All right. Four weeks from there."

"My. An expert on a woman's cycle."

He met her eyes. He wasn't smiling. "This is a stupid game."

"I'm not the one who insisted on playing it."

"Is there some reason you don't want me to

know? Some reason for keeping me—for keeping both of us—in the dark?''

The question got snagged in her mind and wouldn't shake loose. She felt a tiny stab—a pinprick, a needle's jab—at her conscience.

The day after a missed period, the brochure had said. According to that, they could know on Saturday. In four days, her life could be irrevocably changed.

Yes, she did realize that if it *was* changed, it had happened already. It had happened almost two weeks ago in a small green clearing in the strange half light of a Gullandrian summer night. No home pregnancy test would change what already was.

Still...

The simple truth was as Finn had just said. She didn't *want* to know. Not yet. As soon as she knew— as soon as *Finn* knew—decisions would have to be made.

Oh, not yet, her heart cried. *Don't make me decide yet.*

So strange, for her, Liv Thorson, to be thinking of her heart. She didn't go there, as a rule. She dated men like dear, sweet Simon. They told each other they *cared* for each other—and they did. They worked hard to excel. They spent their evenings studying or rallying for social change or discussing America's rights and responsibilities as the only true remaining world superpower, debating this or that issue currently before the Supreme Court.

It was nothing like this magic, this enchantment, with Finn. Yes, she'd had sex before that one unforgettable night with Finn. But not often, and not for a while. Until Finn, she simply hadn't seen what all the shouting was about.

She and the men she'd known before didn't kiss endlessly on porch swings and whisper of romantic movies and tell each other what it was like back when they were children. They didn't share picnics in Pioneer Park. They'd had more *important* things to do.

And it wasn't that she didn't value all the same things that had mattered to her before. She did value them, and highly. It was only that she was seeing a whole new side of herself, one that, until Finn, she'd left utterly unexplored.

Her mother had said it the night Liv found Finn staying at Ingrid's house. The stop-and-smell-the-flowers part of her needed room to grow. And Finn Danelaw knew better than anyone how to help her with that.

He'd done, she decided, a wonderful job of helping her so far, in spite of how she'd fought him every inch of the way. She wouldn't mind at all if he kept helping her, indefinitely—for as long as the magic lasted between them.

However, just because she wanted something didn't make it fair or right. Finn couldn't be expected to hang around in California forever making certain that Liv Thorson had a good time. She had no right to string him along for one minute beyond the day when they'd both know for certain if there'd be a baby or not.

From the first time he'd proposed, that Sunday morning in Gullandria, she'd told him she'd take a test as soon as she could. It was only fair, only right, that she do as she'd promised. Only fair that he should know when that time would be.

Liv snatched the calendar from him and threw it over her shoulder. It hit the heavy oak door behind her and slid to the shining hardwood floor.

He looked puzzled but not especially surprised. "No need to start throwing things."

She said, "My period is due Friday. If it doesn't come, I'll take the test Saturday morning."

Chapter Ten

Finn reached out and slipped his fingers around the back of her neck. He gave a tug—a tender one. It didn't take more than that. He was, after all, only pulling her where she wanted to go.

She landed with a sigh against him.

He lowered his mouth so that it just brushed hers. "Was that so difficult?"

"Yes."

"Why?"

She glanced away.

"Look at me."

She made herself do that. "I just realized I'm going to hate saying goodbye to you."

He kissed her, quick and hard. "You won't have to. You'll be coming with me."

She shook her head. "I can't do that, Finn. You

know I can't. Not and continue with the plans I've made for myself. I can't be in politics in California—if I live in Gullandria.''

He asked tenderly, "You want that so very much, to run this state of yours someday?"

"Oh, Finn. I do. I want…to make a difference. I want to leave the world a better place than it was when I got here."

"There are other ways to do that than to be a governor or a senator."

"You're right, there are."

He chuckled. "Say that again—the part about how I'm right."

She wrinkled up her nose at him. "Okay. *You're right*. There *are* other ways. But those other ways aren't *my* way."

He looked at her deeply. "Maybe you'll reconsider. Maybe you'll…how do you say it? Rearrange your priorities."

"Maybe *you'll* move to America."

"I am Gullandrian." He wasn't smiling.

She wasn't smiling, either. "And I am American."

"We have a problem."

She nodded. "We do—or we might. It could, after all, turn out that I'm not even pregnant."

He was studying her again, giving her that feeling that he could see down into her soul. "You're saying that everything would be solved if you're not pregnant?"

Would it?

Uh-uh.

With humor and heat and relentless tenderness, this man had left his mark on her. She would never forget him, whatever they found out when she took that test.

"No," she confessed on a breath. "It wouldn't. Not everything. If I'm not pregnant, you'll leave. I might never see you again. And I'll miss you, so very much."

He lifted a hand, traced the line of her hair where it fell along her cheek. "Four days, until Saturday…"

She felt a pang of sadness, sharp and also infinitely sweet. "It's no time at all."

"True." His eyes glittered down at her. She could feel every glorious, lean male inch of him pressing so close. And all she wanted was to have him closer still.

She lifted up, brushed her mouth once, and then again, across his. "Let's not waste a moment."

He whispered, almost as if it hurt him to say it, "Such willingness suddenly."

She kissed his chin with its faint, masculine cleft. "Not so sudden. We both know you've been breaking me down for days now."

"Breaking you down?" His eyes were hooded.

"Oh, you know you have. With your endless stunning kisses, with your hand that won't stop reaching for my hand, with the way you listen, as if mine is the only voice you'll ever hear." She laughed, low in her throat. "But I know all the women must tell you that."

He gave her a smile—a faint one, the smallest hitch at both sides of his mouth. "How would I know, as yours is the only voice I hear?"

"Hmm. A question I don't think we need to even try to answer."

"Wisely said."

She put a finger to his mouth, felt the feathery warm caress of his breath against her palm. He caught her hand, kissed the fingertips and then guided it up to encircle his neck.

"Such softness," he whispered, his mouth against hers again, "and pressed so close…"

"And we shouldn't waste a minute, a second, a *fraction* of a second…"

His hand swept down her back. He tucked her snugly into him. She felt the firm ridge of his erection against her lower belly. And then he was kissing her—little, brushing butterfly kisses—up over her cheek to her ear.

He smoothed her hair out of his way and he whispered, "What would you like, my darling?" He captured her earlobe and worried it tenderly between his teeth.

"Oh!" She lifted her hips, pressing in shamelessly, making a cradle for him. "Everything."

"Everything?"

"Oh, yes. Please."

He took her face between his two hands and claimed her mouth—hard—his teeth punishing her lips. She moaned.

He softened the kiss, teasing her mouth with his questing tongue, running it over the bow of her upper lip, tracing the slightly fuller bottom lip until she moaned again.

He caught her lower lip between his teeth gently, dragging on it. "Open for me."

With a small cry, she obeyed. His tongue slid in, slick and wet and wonderful. He swept all her inner surfaces, claiming them, branding them as his, leaving a hot trail of longing in his wake.

Liv was melting, sighing, gone already. And all he'd done was kiss her.

He turned her, one hand sliding down to catch her under the knees, one bracing across the widest part of her back. She shuddered as her feet left the floor.

His tongue moved in her mouth, thrusting, retreating and thrusting again, in a blatant imitation of the motions of lovemaking. He started up the stairs carrying her high in his arms, never once breaking the hot rhythm of the shamelessly sexual kiss. At the top, he lifted his mouth just enough to ask ''Which room?''

She flung out a hand toward her open bedroom door and dragged his head back down to hers. Four steps and they were there.

Somehow, he turned her—how did he do those things?—and guided her legs to wrap around his waist. She kicked off her sandals. One and then the other, they thudded against the wall. She hooked her bare feet at the small of his back, locking herself around him like a vine around a tree.

She kissed him deep and hard and oh so wet.

Images spun and pulsed through her mind: wet things, open things—orchids beaded with dewdrops, the secret, moist sweetness of a freshly cut peach. She saw slick curves…a large, thick glass vase, calla lilies standing in it, water cascading down the sides of it, dripping more gently on the flowers themselves.

The flowers, so white, velvety trumpets dewed

with water drops like jewels, naughty stamens like tongues...

He already had her button-front sundress scrunched up around her waist. He cradled her thighs on his lean arms, those incredible hands of his cupping her bottom, fingers slipping skillfully under the elastic of her panties, finding her, spreading her, gliding along her cleft, which was already thoroughly drenched, swollen with yearning. Liv writhed and moaned and kept on kissing him.

She had a sensation of opening, of turning, wet flower petals blooming so wide that the inside turned outside. His fingers teased her, readied her, while his manhood pressed up, hard, insistent, shielded from her by his clothing and her panties. She could have stayed there forever, in the doorway, wrapped all around him, kissing him endlessly, her body moving, pulsing, yearning, in his strong arms.

But he had other plans. Still kissing her, he lowered her. She slid down his body with a needful moan.

He fisted his hand in her hair and he tugged, gently, inexorably, until the kiss broke.

"Liv," he said. "Ah, Liv..." He scraped his teeth along her chin, his fist opening, his hand easing from her hair.

Her head tipped back, her eyes still closed, she drew in one slow breath. And another.

There. She was able to open her eyes and lift her head.

The sight of him thrilled her, his eyes so hot they seemed to burn her, his mouth as swollen as hers— swollen and hot, as if every nerve had been drawn to the surface, the flesh itself seeming to cry out for the next consuming kiss.

He laid a hand between her breasts, at the top button of her sundress. Light as a breath, his fingers went to work. The button fell open. Then the next, and the next....

He was still fully dressed. She could help him with that. She got to work, starting at the top button of his shirt, staring in his eyes as she slipped each button from its hole.

But then she happened to glance down. The front of her dress, with its built-in demibra, gaped open. Her nipples, drawn to tight buds, were exposed.

"So pretty," he whispered, as he took a nipple between thumb and forefinger and rolled it.

She moaned. And he edged the sides of the dress farther apart, both hands at work now, guiding the thin straps over her shoulders and down.

The dress fell away. She stood before him in only her panties. He knelt, taking hold of that scrap of satin and lace and whisking it over her hips, along her thighs.

She stared down at him, slightly stunned. She'd never seen his eyes so soft. So hot. Like fire. Amber fire.

She thought of that other night, a continent and an ocean away. Of the sleek Viking ship, blazing, the flames reflected in his eyes...

Her panties were all the way down, at her ankles. She stepped out of them. His hands moved back up, along the outsides of her calves, over her knees and then inward. Her thighs trembled. She had to clasp his strong shoulders to brace herself upright.

The brushing caress turned searingly intimate, his palms against the front of her, thumbs burrowing in, dragging in the wetness, rubbing back and forth, back and forth...

Liv groaned. Her eyes would not stay open.

He was leaning closer. She felt the heat of his breath—and then his lips upon her. She cried out then. He wrapped his hands around her hips, pulling her into him, opening her with his hot, skilled mouth, delving in with his clever, knowing tongue.

He found her, found the center of her pleasure, the small, swollen nub tucked away in the wet folds. He drew on it.

She clutched his shoulders and moaned. She couldn't bear it. Couldn't...

Words blew away. The world spun off into twilight and wonder. She saw meadows, smelled heather and cedar, felt the acrid tang of wood smoke at the back of her throat. And there was fire. Endless, red fire, blazing toward the twilit sky.

She called his name and the pulsing began. He held her to him as the contractions claimed her, his mouth tender and demanding, never letting go.

At the end, she crumpled on a groan. He let her fall, guiding her so she dropped across his shoulder, limp, finished.

She let out another sharp cry of surprise as he rose beneath her. The floor moved away and she found herself carried, head down, legs dangling, like the ravished prize from some hard-fought midnight raid. He wrapped an arm tight around her to steady her. A few dizzying steps and they reached the bed.

''Here we are.'' He was whispering, the sounds

soothing, coaxing. Carefully, as if she were a most precious burden, he lowered her to her back on the high, soft mattress. Then he stood to his height again and looked down at her.

She lay under his gaze, without a stitch on, arms and legs flung luxuriously out, everything heavy—with heat, with stunned satisfaction. She had no urge to move or to cover herself.

He looked at her, at all of her, his gaze burning. She felt claimed by him, *his* in some deep and irrevocable way.

She had felt this same soul-deep sense of possession Midsummer's Eve in Gullandria. And as soon as the morning came, she'd set herself to escape it—to escape *him*.

It hadn't worked out the way she'd planned.

Really, the truth was, it hadn't worked out at all.

He had won this race. And in this at least—in her passion for him—she conceded to him willingly.

With a soft sigh, she lifted her arms.

He started undressing, quickly, ruthlessly, kicking off his shoes, tearing off his socks, shrugging his shirt off and tossing it behind him, yanking his zipper down, shoving his pants and briefs off in the same motion. He stared at her the whole time, pausing only to take from a pocket a few small foil pouches, the condoms he'd forgotten that other night.

She smiled at that. "Prepared this time, huh?"

He gave no answer. She gazed up at him. He was so tall and lean, every muscle sharply defined, long rather than bulging. Graceful, in a thoroughly masculine way. A dusting of chestnut hair tracked the center of his chest, continued over his lean belly, and widened to a nest between his strong thighs. His manhood stood out, proof of his intent. She looked at the strong, upthrusting shaft, and then she looked back into his eyes. Her smile trembled. Her whole body felt as if it shimmered in sheer eagerness.

He tossed the last of his clothing aside and joined her on the bed, settling himself between her open thighs, lifting up enough to slide the protection into place. She lowered a hand and took him, guiding him home.

He lunged deep, filling her. She gasped in shocked delight, grasping his hard shoulders, holding on tight.

He moved—a slow, rocking motion, settling in. Then he rested on his forearms above her and sought her eyes.

It was Midsummer's Eve again. They were joined, they didn't move. He looked into her, into the heart of her. And she looked back at him.

"Sweet," he whispered. "So very sweet."

She sighed and managed a nod. "Oh, yes."

Time spun out, a web of stillness and sensation. She couldn't have named the exact moment when they began to move. It happened so slowly, her body responding to his, so they rippled together, a seamless swaying, like waves lapping on a gentle sea.

His eyes changed. They made demands of her. She gave herself up to them—gave herself up to *him,* as the rhythm below became faster, deeper, frantic....

Needful.

She wrapped her arms and legs around him, anchoring on him, and drew him down. He buried his silky head in her shoulder.

The rhythm slowed, each stroke so long and hot

and deep. And then, with a groan, he was moving faster again, she with him.

She saw the heavens, exploding on the inside of her eyelids, stars going supernova, everything shimmering, a blanket of light thrown out to swallow the universe.

A sense of falling.

Of opening.

Lilies, roses, water...

Heat.

Liv heard a shout of pure erotic joy. Several endless moments went by before she recognized it as her own.

Chapter Eleven

"Come home with me tomorrow," he whispered. "We'll be married in the Viking way."

"Oh, Finn. I *am* home."

He looked at her for a long time. She wasn't sure she liked what she saw in his eyes. Finally he covered her mouth with his own in a savage, demanding kiss.

She didn't fight him. She wrapped her arms around his neck and kissed him right back, as hard as he was kissing her. Slowly, the kiss gentled.

And then it turned to heat and hunger.

They spoke no more of marriage that night.

They got up much later, showered together and went out for a late meal. He stayed with her until morning.

It was after nine when Finn returned to Ingrid's house. Hilda came out on the back steps as he was emerging from his rental car. The housekeeper watched him, her long face set in a scowl as he came across the lawn.

"Well," he said cheerfully, "good morning to you, too."

Hilda grunted. She opened the screen door and held it for him to go through.

"Thank you, Hilda."

"Humph," said the housekeeper.

"Is Ingrid already gone for the day?"

Another grumbling sound. He assumed it must mean yes.

Finn turned and faced her once she'd joined him on the big service porch. "Something you'd like to say to me, Hilda?"

One side of her thin lip lifted in an expression very close to a sneer. "His Majesty called for you ten minutes ago. He asked if you'd returned yet. I said you were...still out. He said to tell you to call him back as soon as you got in."

"All right. And you're angry because His Majesty called?"

"I am only a servant," the housekeeper said, aggressively humble.

Finn knew that when good servants got surly, it was usually wisest to keep after them until they admitted what was bothering them, and then to immediately take pains to solve the problem. Otherwise, they tended to exercise their pent-up frustrations in inconvenient and unpleasant ways—they'd run off with the silver, or take to spitting in the soup.

"Come on, hit me with your best shot." He smiled

to himself. He liked that expression. It came from an old song by an American rock star, Pat Benatar, a song that sounded especially satisfying when played very loud.

"Too much scheming around here of late," the housekeeper muttered. "The king knows where you've been. So does the queen. So do *I*."

"And?"

The housekeeper shook her iron-gray head. "I don't like it, that's all. I'm not so blind as some. I have no stars in my eyes at the idea of a grandchild. I know what Liv wants from life. And I can see it's not at all what you have planned for her. I know the ways of Gullandria. I know you will see to it, in the end, that she marries you—whatever you have to do to make it happen."

"You know then why I'm here?"

Hilda knew. The servants always did. "Liv has shown the Freyasdahl signs. She carries your child."

"And you are Gullandrian by birth?" He knew she was.

She admitted it. "I am."

"Then you should understand why a marriage has become imperative."

"I understand more than you think. Liv is not like Elli. She's not a woman to follow her man wherever he must go. You think to tame her to your will. Think again."

Finn stared into Hilda's piercing dark eyes. He wondered if perhaps she'd been raised among the Mystics.

A chill crept up his spine.

And why in the name of all the frozen towers of

Hel was he standing here explaining himself to the housekeeper? He'd do better to leave her to spit in the soup.

"Thank you for the advice, Hilda."

Hilda took his meaning. The subject was closed. She brought a fist to her chest in the Gullandrian salute of respect for one's betters. "Will you have breakfast, sir?"

"I'll go up and make that call. I'll be down in an hour to eat, if that's convenient."

"Of course. I'll have it ready."

"Well?" said the king.

"Your Majesty, I am returning your call."

"Stating the obvious is not answering my question. I know you spent the night with my daughter."

"Sire."

"Has she come to her senses?"

"If you mean, has she agreed to a marriage—no, she has not."

"Is it your intention to stay there in America forever, catering to her every whim?"

Finn decided that silence was the most effective answer to that one.

The king sighed. "In the end, you know, you'll have to take her."

Finn was thinking that Osrik Thorson, given his own marital situation, was the last person he ought to be listening to when it came to the question of what to do about a woman.

But one did not remind one's king of such things. "I'll do what I must do, my lord."

"Has she at least admitted there is a child?"

"No, my lord. But that time is coming."

"When?"

"Very soon."

That night, Liv took Finn to the Convention Center to hear the Lieutenant Governor speak on preserving coastal ecology. A five-hundred-dollar-a-plate fund-raising dinner followed. Liv and Finn found themselves seated at the same table as the state treasurer and his wife. When he learned Finn was Gullandrian, the treasurer asked him a few questions about the new European currency. Finn explained that Gullandria, like the other Scandinavian countries, was sticking with its national currency, the Gullandrian *krone*. They spoke of the offshore oil industry. Finn said that, because of it, the Gullandrian standard of living was much higher than it had once been.

The treasurer's wife wanted to hear of the recent wedding of Liv's sister. So Liv and Finn took turns describing a Viking wedding.

It was well after midnight when they returned to the T Street house. They paused on the porch for a long, searching kiss.

Then she slipped the key in the lock and pushed open the door. "Will you...come in?"

He swept her high in his arms and carried her inside, kicking the door shut behind him.

The next day was the Fourth of July. Ingrid, Liv and Finn went together to the picnic sponsored by the Boys and Girls Clubs of Sacramento. There was softball. Liv and Finn played on opposite teams. Twice, Finn put her out at third.

That night, after the fireworks at the fairgrounds and the more intimate pyrotechnics at home, she told him she didn't at all appreciate the look of pleasure on his face those two times he caught the ball just as she was sliding in.

He pulled her close and kissed her hard. "Ah, my love. Leave a man his petty triumphs, won't you?"

"Why? Your team won."

For that, she got a maddening low chuckle.

She grumbled, "I'll bet you're a lousy loser."

"Not as lousy as you are, my darling." He slid beneath the sheet, disappearing from her view. She felt the shivery scrape of his tongue against the curve of her hip. "I am not a lousy loser," she announced.

And then she moaned.

And then she forgot everything but the magic he could work with his hands and his tongue.

Liv and a number of other "nonessential" staff at the Justice Department got Friday off.

She and Finn slept late. When they woke, they made leisurely love. Then they wandered downstairs and fixed a big brunch, which they ate sitting on the floor in the family room watching daytime TV, sharing coffee-flavored kisses.

Later they went over to Old Sac. They strolled the wooden sidewalks and toured the permanently moored *Delta King*. When Ingrid's shop closed at six, they took her to dinner.

They were back at the T Street house by eight-thirty—and wrapped in each other's arms upstairs in her bed by nine. They made love and then they made love again.

They slept.

Live woke a little after two. She looked at the clock and she thought of the test she'd agreed to take in just a few short hours. The truth was, the test had been there, lurking in the back of her mind, since the night Finn had brought it to her and they became lovers again.

Her period hadn't come and she'd experienced none of the usual signs that it *was* coming. Still, things had been stressful, to say the least, these past few weeks. In all likelihood, she was simply going to be a little late this month.

She turned her head and looked at the sleeping man beside her, resisting the all-too-constant urge to touch him, to trace his fine brows, to brush at his hair where it curled at his temple, to run her finger down his beautiful blade of a nose.

Positive or negative...

Either way, tomorrow she would probably lose him. Unless she agreed to return to Gullandria and become his wife. The choice, in the end, was one she dreaded having to make. Give him up. Or give up her dreams for herself.

There was pressure at the back of her throat. Ridiculous. She was Liv Thorson, head of her class, with a mind like a steel trap. She was going into politics and there was no crying in politics. She swallowed to banish the traitorous tightness.

Finn stirred. He opened his eyes. Through the darkness she saw the white flash of his smile. The smile faded and he looked at her deeply as he realized what was going through her mind. "Don't think about it. Plenty of time for that when daylight comes.''

She did touch him, then. She laid her palm against his cheek, rough now with the beginnings of morning stubble. ''It seems as if we've just begun to get to know each other.''

''Come home with me. Marry me.''

What could she say? She settled for snuggling close and lifting her mouth to his.

Daylight came too quickly, a golden slice of light between the curtains. Finn lay with his eyes closed as he felt the bed shift.

Oh, he knew her. Three short weeks since the night he'd first seen her, in the grand ballroom at Isenhalla, a frown on her kissable mouth as she watched him whirl another across the floor. Two weeks since Midsummer's Eve, when he'd first held her naked in his arms. And but a few short days since he'd become her lover once again.

The blankets moved slightly as she slid from the bed. Her bare feet whispered across the floor. The bathroom door made hardly a sound as she shut it behind her.

He turned so that he could watch the clock. The test would take several minutes. He waited.

When the time came, he pushed back the covers and rose from the bed. He knew she wouldn't lock the door.

She hadn't. He turned the handle and pushed it open. And there she was, wearing a fluffy white robe, perched on the edge of the claw-footed tub, head bent over the test wand, her straight gold hair sleep-tangled, falling forward over her shoulders.

Something happened inside him right then as he stood naked in the doorway and stared at the vulnerable crown of her head. Something tore.

Something ripped wide open.

She looked up. Her face was white as her robe, the blue eyes haunted.

Up till now, he'd been able to keep his eyes on the prize—the prize being to get the mother of his child to marry him and come home with him where she belonged. *My love,* he had called her. And *Darling Liv.* It had all been in the nature of a delicious game, a game he had played for the joy and the challenge of it, his only goal: to win.

But all at once it was a game no longer. His mouth tasted of ashes as he recognized the moment for what it was: the moment of his own defeat.

"Well?" The word emerged from his mouth sounding harsh, guttural.

She whispered, "I'm pregnant."

It was no surprise to Finn. He'd known she carried his child from the Sunday after Midsummer's Eve, when her father called him to his chambers to tell him of the Freyasdahl signs and their meaning.

No, it wasn't the news of a baby coming that stole his breath and gripped his belly to a fisted knot.

It was the sudden clear knowledge that he loved her.

Deeply.

Completely.

He loved her in a way he had never, ever meant to love anyone—the way his father had once loved his mother, the way that cut out all others and left him longing only for her.

He felt scraped raw, his flesh peeled away. Leaving him much worse than naked. Leaving him shamed and revealed: the seducer, seduced.

He looked into those stunned blue eyes and saw her doubts, her thousand and one denials. He knew her thoughts exactly. "You never believed you were pregnant, did you, until now?"

She swallowed, her slim throat moving convulsively, and she shook her head.

"And even though you know it now, you *still* don't plan to marry me, do you?"

She found her voice. She used it to sputter excuses, to stammer out halting evasions. "It's just...so difficult. To believe. I, well, of course, somehow there'll be a way. It's going to be...challenging, but not impossible."

He knew what people called him. Player. Charmer. A man who changed lovers like most men change shirts. And it was true. He wanted to give pleasure. And take it. It was never his intention to love anyone too much or too long. He'd seen what that could do to a man.

Yet at the core he was Gullandrian. It was bred in the bone with him to make certain his children were born only to his wife.

What a vain, proud fool he'd been. He should have taken the advice of his king, should have kidnapped her that morning when she first refused him, should have kept her under lock and key until she'd agreed to marry him and the baby was born.

Then, Freyja curse her, she could have divorced

him. What would it have mattered? His child would have his name; the goal would be won.

Yes, Liv would have hated him, but he wouldn't have cared. Not in any deep way. He would hardly know her, after all. She wouldn't have *let* him know her, had she been his captive. Not a woman like Liv. She'd have fought him every step of the way.

But no. He couldn't simply take her and be done with it. He'd had to do it *his* way. He'd thought himself the smooth one, the one who understood the twenty-first century woman so well.

And now what? Now that her eyes told him so clearly, so regretfully, that she would never marry him. How in the name of all the nine worlds would he bring himself to carry her off and imprison her at Balmarran? Now that he loved her. Now that her happiness and high regard meant everything to him, more, even, than the right of his child to be born legitimate.

"By Odin's one eye, just say it," he demanded low. "Just tell me. Once and for all. Will you marry me?"

"Oh, Finn. You know I can't. I...I have things I...what I mean is, I just don't think..."

Before she could finish stuttering out her refusal, he turned and left her there.

"Finn!" Liv jumped up to follow as he disappeared into the other room. She took one step and faltered. The wand that proved she was pregnant was still in her hand. She looked down at it, shook her head and dropped to the edge of the tub once more.

Finn had been right. She had never really believed. Until now.

In the other room, she could hear him moving around. She didn't understand his strange, abrupt reaction. It was so unlike him. Of the two of them, he was always the reasonable, levelheaded one. He took everything in stride, with a wink and smile and a clever remark.

She ought to get in there and talk to him, find out what was going on with him, but right at that moment, she was in no condition to find out anything. Right at that moment, she was, quite simply, reeling.

A baby...

It didn't seem possible. It wasn't...in the plan.

Liv wasn't the one who was going to have the *babies*. Not for years and years yet. Elli was the one who'd have all the kids. In any case, Elli was supposed to have three or four of them before Liv got around to deciding if, just maybe, she dared to add a baby to all the other heavy responsibilities that would come with her powerhouse career.

A baby came under the heading: *Hope so. Eventually.*

After I'm established...

If I find the right husband, a nice, settled-down type of guy, a guy willing to change diapers and get up close and personal with the downside of parenthood: things like colic and late-night feedings, ferrying them around as they got older, taking them to the pediatrician and the orthodontist, checking into the best schools, monitoring their homework, making sure they ate right...

God. The list went on and on.

True, she'd been telling herself for two weeks that

she *might* be pregnant. That *maybe* it was something she'd have to come to grips with soon.

But *might* and *maybe* were worlds away from the two solid blue lines in the little white wand.

It was real. It was going to happen. She was having a baby.

She tossed the wand into the trash and then sat there some more, hunched on the tub's edge, staring at the bath mat beneath her bare feet.

The sound of the door shutting downstairs brought her up straight.

Finn must have left.

She sighed and let her shoulders droop again. In a while, later today, she'd give him a call. Ask him to come back over. They'd talk about it, about...

Well, she wasn't sure exactly what yet. She was on *overwhelm* right at the moment.

She got up and went back to the bedroom. She climbed into the bed and pulled the sheet over herself and told herself she'd feel better about everything in a little while.

The ringing of the phone woke her. She almost let her service get it, but then realized it might be Finn.

She fumbled on the nightstand and brought it to her ear. "Yeah? Hello."

"Liv, are you *sleeping?*" It was Ingrid, in a thoroughly accusatory mood. "You sound like you're *sleeping.*"

Liv scrambled to a sitting position and raked her hair back out of her eyes. "Mother, what's the—"

"Finn has gone back to Gullandria. He simply packed his bags and left."

Chapter Twelve

"I don't understand it," Ingrid cried. "Did you have a fight, is that it?"

Liv was having a little trouble absorbing this. "Mom. Wait. Tell me what happened. What did he say?"

"I really thought the two of you were getting along so well. I thought—"

"We were. We *are.*"

"Well then, what went wrong?"

"Look. Will you please just tell me what happened?"

"Well, he came in. He went upstairs. About twenty minute later, he came through the kitchen loaded down with all his bags. He thanked me for my hospitality. He said it was time he went back where he belonged."

Liv just didn't get it. It all seemed unreal, the way he'd walked out on her earlier. And now this, taking off for Gullandria without even saying goodbye to her.

Ingrid continued. "I followed him out to his car, under the pretext of seeing him off. I asked if there was a problem, something wrong between the two of you...."

Liv gulped. "And?"

"He told me not to worry. That everything was fine. And then he thanked me again and said he had to leave." Ingrid made a small sound of distress. "Darling, please. You can tell me. Did you have a fight?"

"No. We didn't. Honestly."

"But then what could be wrong?"

Liv didn't know. And if her mother kept grilling her, she was going to scream. "Mom. I can't...talk about it right now. I have to go."

"Are you all right?"

"Fine. Really. I just have to go."

After another volley of frantic protests and pleading questions, Ingrid finally gave up and said goodbye.

Liv turned off the phone and yanked the sheet over her head. She'd go to sleep. She'd sleep all day and right through into the next night. As long as she was sleeping, she wouldn't have to think about what the heck she ought to do next.

But sleep played its usual tricks. Naturally, since she longed for it so much, it refused to come.

After an hour or so of staring at the underside of the sheet, she got up and made breakfast. She sat at the table in the kitchen alone and wished Finn was there. She missed him already. She also wanted a chance to yell at him for walking out on her like this.

And wasn't that just like a player? The going gets tough and the player gets lost.

Maybe she should have given him a real reason to run. When he asked her to marry him that last time, in the bathroom this morning, she should have looked him square in the eye and said yes.

But of course, she couldn't.

A marriage between them was never going to work. She had her education to finish here in America, and after that, years and years worth of important goals to accomplish. And he had his castle, his troublesome sister, his long-suffering grandfather and his legions of feminine admirers in Gullandria. And never the twain shall meet, as they say.

He was a gorgeous hunk of man and she would miss him.

But maybe it was for the best that he was gone. She needed to start getting used to the idea that he wouldn't be around forever, that he wasn't the kind of man she could count on. And now, with a baby to think of, on top of all the rest of it, a man she could count on was the only kind she had any business getting near. Liv rinsed her dishes and put them in the dishwasher and went upstairs to take a shower.

A few hours later, she called her mother and explained that yes, even *she* believed she was pregnant now. And she wanted Ingrid to accept the fact that she wasn't, under any circumstances, going to be marrying Finn. Finn had said it himself: he'd gone back to where he belonged. She wished him well.

And now she planned to get on with her life.

Finn flew to Gullandria in His Majesty's Gulf-stream.

The jet had been right there, waiting, at Executive Airport, during the entire two weeks Finn had spent in America. The king had ordered it to remain on standby in anticipation of the happy moment when Finn would bring his bride back home.

Instead, he boarded alone. Within an hour they were cleared for takeoff.

It was 3:20 a.m. when they touched down in a cool, misty Gullandrian semidarkness.

Finn was getting off the plane when Hauk Wyborn stepped up to him. "His Majesty would speak with you, Prince Danelaw. This way."

It was not a good sign when the king's warrior appeared to escort a man to the king. But Finn didn't object. His objections wouldn't change a thing and a meeting with the king—destined, no doubt, to be un-pleasant—was inevitable, in any case.

The black car was waiting. Finn ducked into it and Hauk slid in behind him.

Hauk spoke to the driver and they were off, rolling across the tarmac toward the road. Through the tinted windows, Finn spotted the knot of reporters not far from the gate that led to the terminal. How sad for them. Up so early on the scent of a story, and Hauk had herded him into the car before they got a chance to snap their pictures and shout the usual thoroughly intrusive questions.

Finn turned to the giant warrior beside him. "You look well, Hauk. I'd say marriage agrees with you."

Hauk allowed one dip of his big golden head. "Yes. I am indeed a fortunate man."

Finn let his mouth twist into a wry grin. "Let me take this, er, rare opportunity to congratulate you."

"Thank you."

The warrior stared forward. Finn did the same. The car cut through the windless misty night.

At the palace, Hauk made himself scarce once he'd escorted Finn to the king's private audience room.

Osrik was waiting for him, resplendent, even at four in the morning, in a fine gray pinstripe designer suit with a red tie. Medwyn stood nearby.

"Prince Danelaw," said the king. "Welcome." His stern expression belied the word of greeting.

"Your Majesty." Finn saluted.

"You surprise us," said the king. "Back so abruptly. Without forewarning. And without my daughter."

"Yes, Your Majesty," said Finn, because he felt some sort of response was called for, though, in fact, he had nothing at all to say.

"What news do you have for us?"

"Sire, none at all. It was time I came home, that's all. Once full daylight comes, I'll go on to Balmarran. I want to check on my sister, assure myself that she hasn't yet managed to drive my poor grandfather mad."

The king, wearing an expression that was far from benign, studied Finn for several endless seconds. At last he said, "My daughter. Has she agreed to marry you, then?"

"No, my lord. She hasn't. She's said no repeatedly. I've become quite certain that no is what she means."

"She won't agree to marry you—ever?"

"That's right, sire."

"You're sure of this?"

"I am."

The king frowned. "Are you telling me, then, that the Freyasdahl signs have been proven wrong in her case?"

"No, Your Majesty. Your daughter carries my child."

"And she won't marry you. She refuses. You're certain of this?"

"I am."

The king heaved a deep sigh. "Then it's as I told you from the first. You will have to take her." The king paused, waiting for Finn to agree with him. Finn didn't. The king looked at him darkly and went on. "It will be more difficult now that she's back in America. You should have listened to me, Finn. She'd be at Balmarran now."

"It doesn't matter."

The king's frowned deepened. "Doesn't matter? What's this? Of course it matters."

"I don't intend to take her."

The king stood very still. "What did you say?" His deep voice vibrated with barely leashed fury.

"I said, sire, that she's chosen not to marry me. She wants to stay in America and raise the child on her own. I think she'll make a fine mother. Your wife, the queen, will make certain she has everything she needs. Liv—and my child—will thrive."

A rumble of rage rose from the king's throat. "You would make of your own child a fitz."

Finn kept his face resolutely expressionless. "It's America. The child will suffer little stigma there. And I refuse to claim a wife against her will."

There was a moment of echoing silence. The king looked at him as if he had lost his mind. And maybe he had.

Then the king commanded, "You will go for her. You will take her. You will keep her until she's wed you and the child is born."

"I am sorry, Your Majesty. But no. I will not."

Liv's phone rang in the deepest part of the night.

She bolted upright in bed and cried out, "Finn!" before she came fully awake and remembered he was gone and she was getting over him.

She grabbed the receiver on the third ring and barked into it, "What?"

A crackle of static, then Brit's voice. "Don't tell me I woke you."

"It's two in the morning here, did you know that!"

"Well, yes. I admit, I did. But I've been... developing my sources around here."

Liv wasn't getting it. "Your *sources?*"

"All right, I'll be crass. My spies. I have spies of my own now. Believe me, around here I need them— and Elli's here."

"With you?"

"Uh-huh. I'll put her on in a minute."

"Okay. Good—spies? You have spies?"

"You got it."

"So, you have news for me, is that it? From these spies of yours?"

"Yes. And Elli confirms it."

"Confirms what?"

"That father's had Finn Danelaw thrown into Tarngalla."

Tarngalla. Liv couldn't believe it. "You're not serious."

"Oh, but I am."

Liv recalled her first sight of the stone fortress about ten miles north of Lysgard, on a treeless stretch of land. The edifice itself had looked impenetrable, its forbidding aspect made more so by the high electrified fence surrounding it, coils of cruel barbed wire on top.

Finn had been with her that day. "Watch your step," he'd warned. "Do murder and get caught, perpetrate a dastardly crime against the state—and Tarngalla awaits. Parents of naughty children have invoked its specter for centuries now. 'Keep up like that, young man, and it's Tarngalla for you...'"

Liv was suddenly wide-awake. "Father threw Finn in *prison?*"

"Isn't that what I just said?"

"But why?"

"We don't know yet."

"We?"

"Me. Elli—we're trying to find out."

"Did you ask Father?"

"It was only early this morning that it happened, from what we've been able to piece together. Dad has been unavailable since then."

"I'll bet," Liv muttered.

Brit said, "Elli and I got together on it. We decided we ought to let you in on the situation."

"I can't believe it. Finn in prison. Are you sure?"

"I heard it from more than one source before I tried to get in to see Dad. Elli heard about it from Hauk—she'll explain that in a minute. Anyway, she and I have been talking. We figured you'd be interested—given the reports that you two are in love, engaged and getting married any minute."

"Don't believe everything you read in *The World Tattler*."

"But he *was* there, right? Staying with Mom, hanging around with you on a daily basis?"

"Yes."

"And I—" Brit cut herself off. "Okay, okay..." Her voice had grown slightly fainter, as if she'd stopped speaking into the mouthpiece. She must be talking to Elli. Then she spoke into the receiver again. "Hold on."

"Liv?" Suddenly it was Elli's voice in her ear. "Are you okay? Brit says...there's a baby."

Liv's throat felt tight. Maybe it was the pregnancy. She'd be a walking waterworks if she didn't watch herself. "I'm fine. And yes, I'm pregnant. Barely."

"Oh, Livvy..." It was all there in Elli's voice. Joy. Anxiousness. Just a hint of envy—after all, Elli was supposed to be the first one to get pregnant.

"Ell?"

"Um?

"How are *you*?"

"Wonderful. Truly. The happiest woman alive." Even over the phone, her joy in her new life with Hauk came across.

"I'm glad for you."

"Thank you—and about Finn." Elli's voice was all business again. "Let me tell you what I know. Hauk was sent to meet him at the airport with orders to escort him to Father's private chambers. Evidently it didn't go well. Hauk was summoned again, along with two guards that time, to take Finn to Tarngalla."

"But why?"

"Livvy, we don't know. Not for certain."

"What *do* you know?"

"That Finn displeased the king. Greatly. And I think…" The sentence trailed off in the middle.

Liv prompted, "What? Tell me."

"Well, it has to be about you. Hauk met Finn at the plane. Why would father summon him like that, at three in the morning, if not to grill him about you and the baby and you two getting married? Which reminds me…" Elli hesitated, delicately.

Liv made a growling sound. "Oh, go ahead. Ask me."

"*Are* you marrying him?"

"No."

"But why not?"

"Ell, you are such a complete romantic. He lives *there*. I live *here*. Until he found out I was pregnant, we both knew we'd never see each other again. He's not ready for marriage. *I'm* not ready for marriage. We did a stupid thing and now there's a baby on the way and a baby on the way is not reason enough for two people with nothing in common who would otherwise have just walked away from each other to decide they have to spend their lives together. Enough said?''

''Do you love him?''

Liv cast her gaze ceilingward. ''I knew you'd ask that.''

''Love changes everything.''

''I'm sure, for you, it has.''

''You haven't answered my question. Do you love him?''

Did she? And did love even matter in this case? She shook her head. ''It's not the issue.''

''Oh, Livvy. Love is *always* the issue.''

''For you, maybe.''

''And there *is* the baby.''

Liv had her ducks in a row on that one. ''Women have babies on their own all time now. And in my situation, with plenty of money and Mom and Hilda and Granny and the aunts just longing to help out in any way they can? Come on. You know that baby is going to be fine.''

Elli heaved a big sigh. ''Maybe you're right.''

''Of course I'm right.''

''So then, the only one who has to suffer is Finn.''

Liv scowled. ''The implication being that he's in Tarngalla because of me.''

''What other reason can there be? Finn followed you to America to get you to marry him. He failed. So he comes home and he pays the price.''

''Oh, puh-leese. I refuse to marry Finn and *he* gets thrown in jail. Where's the sense in that?''

''Sense has exactly zip to do with it. This is Gullandria. And in Gullandria, if a man doesn't marry the woman who carries his child, there's bound to be

Hel to pay—they may spell it differently, but hell is Hel, you know? Eternal fire or blasted towers of ice, it's big Trouble. Capital T.''

''What it is, is barbaric. Unbelievable. Totally unacceptable.''

''Call it whatever you want. The bottom line is, Finn's in prison. And you're not.''

Liv didn't like the sound of that. ''Wait a minute. Was that some kind of accusation?''

''Of course not. Just a statement of fact, and hold on, Brit wants to say something now.''

Brit came on the line. ''So you're getting the picture?''

''All too clearly.''

''When are you coming?''

''This could royally mess up my internship, you know? First, there was Elli's wedding. I really couldn't afford taking time off for that. It's only a three-month job, after all. If I want the units, I have to—''

''When?''

''I keep asking myself, how can this be happening? How did I get myself into this crazy, impossible, ridiculous—''

''Livvy.''

Liv muttered a very bad word.

''When are you coming?''

''Damn it. As soon as I can find a flight.''

Chapter Thirteen

Liv did have a number where she could supposedly reach her father. He'd given it to her and Brit when he'd had their travel arrangements set up before Elli's wedding. She could have called him and asked him to send one of those royal jets of his to get her. He'd have it ready and waiting for her at Executive Airport in no time. But she couldn't bring herself to speak with him—at least not until she was face-to-face with the man and could deliver the head-on dressing-down he deserved.

So she went online and, for an outrageous price, got a flight out of San Francisco leaving that afternoon at five, nonstop to Heathrow. From there, she'd board a smaller, commuter-type plane for Gullandria.

She packed her bags. By then, it was almost four in the morning. Hours to go until she could do much else and she was far too keyed up to sleep. She paced the floor and tried to read and channel-surfed, all the while thinking of Finn, *aching* for him, hoping he was all right, and mentally rehearsing all the scathing things she'd say to her father.

At eight o'clock, she called the Attorney General's Office and explained that a family emergency had called her away again. No, she didn't know for how long. She sincerely hoped it would only be a few days.

That grim job accomplished, she threw her bags in her car, locked up and went to tell her mother that she was leaving—again.

When Liv burst in the back door, Ingrid and Hildy were sitting in the breakfast nook, having their morning coffee together as they'd done for all the years that Liv could remember.

"Darling," Ingrid exclaimed. "What's happened? You look positively wild."

"I *am* wild." Liv hauled out one of the kitchen chairs and dropped into it. "And I want some coffee, but it's not good for the baby, is it?"

"No darling, I'm afraid it isn't."

"Orange juice?" Hildy offered.

"No thanks. I think I'm going to murder my father. He's a monster and I hate him. He's thrown Finn into Tarngalla, did you know?"

"No, I didn't know." Ingrid sipped her coffee. "But I can't say I'm surprised."

Liv glared at her mother. "How can you be so calm about it?"

"Darling—"

"*Could* you stop calling me that?"

Ingrid blinked. "I've always called you that."

"Well, it reminds me of Finn now. And that...upsets me."

"Ah." Ingrid and Hildy exchanged a look. "Sorry, sweetheart—so you're going to Gullandria?"

"How did you know?"

"Well, what else can you do?"

Liv made a growling sound. "Exactly."

Ingrid and Hildy shared another freighted glance. They did that all the time, carried on private conversations just by looking at each other. Sometimes—like right now—Liv found it irritating in the extreme.

Ingrid said, "Your father is...who he is."

Liv threw up both hands. "You sound like Brit. Next you'll be telling me you and he are reconciling."

Ingrid shook her head. "No. I'm only telling you that nothing you do or say will change Osrik Thorson. And believe me, I know whereof I speak." She set down her cup and leaned closer, across the table. "Livvy, I lost so much. I gave up my sons to keep my daughters, to raise them here, in America, to make certain at least my girls would be safe from that place and all the scheming and dangerous maneuvering for power that goes on there. Yet what's happened? There's an old Norse saying..."

Liv stifled a groan. "Enough with the Norse sayings."

Her mother repeated it anyway. *"The length of my life and the day of my death were fated long ago."*

"Meaning, specifically?"

"What have I accomplished, by fighting my fate? My sons are dead. Perhaps they would have died anyway, but at least, for the years they lived, I would have known them." Blue eyes glistened. Ingrid turned away, collected herself and then faced Liv once more. "And my daughters? Where are my daughters now—the daughters I meant to keep safe from all things Gullandrian? One has married a Gullandrian; one went to Gullandria for a visit and refuses to come home. And one is on her way back to Gullandria just as soon as she can finish telling me goodbye."

Liv put her hand over her mother's. "I'm sorry, Mom."

Ingrid covered Liv's hand, so it was held safe and warm—at least for that moment—between both of hers. She was smiling, a sad little smile. "There is no fighting fate. You and your sisters each have a road to travel. I might have pulled you from your paths temporarily, but now, unerringly, each of you seems to be finding her own road again."

Liv couldn't help asking. She and her sisters had asked so many times and never gotten any real answer. "What happened? Why did you leave him, really? What did he do?"

Ingrid slid her hands free of Liv's and sat back in her chair. "Now is not the time."

"Mom. It's *never* the time."

Hildy cleared her throat. Ingrid glanced toward her lifelong friend. Yet another of those speaking looks passed between them. This time, Liv felt no irritation at the silent communication. She had a clear sense that Hildy was on her side. Hildy wanted Ingrid to reveal at least a little of what had happened all those years ago, what had been so terrible that it had torn their family in two.

Finally Ingrid faced Liv across the table. "Remember, I've told you I had a younger brother who died before you were born?"

Liv nodded. "I remember. His name was Brian."

"Yes. Brian—we all adored him, Nanna and Kirsten and I." They were fraternal triplets, Ingrid and her sisters, just like Ingrid's daughters after them. "Brian was obsessed with all things Gullandrian. When he graduated from high school, he came to stay with us, with Osrik and me and our two sons, at Isenhalla. Osrik was newly crowned then. Kylan was a baby and Valbrand was just three. It was only to be a visit, a few months, in the summer. Brian was set to attend Yale...."

"He wouldn't go back?"

"That's right." Ingrid waved a hand. "Oh, it's a long, sad story."

"Tell me."

After a moment, Liv's mother continued. "Brian wanted, so badly, to become a true Gullandrian. To be accepted by Osrik, by the others at court, as one of the jarl. He badgered Osrik constantly. As king, Osrik had it in his power to make him a citizen, to declare him high jarl. Also, there was the fact that Freyasdahl is an old and respected Gullandrian name, so no one would have argued Brian's right to take his place in the nobility."

"But Father wouldn't grant him citizenship?"

"No. Granny Birget and your grandfather didn't want it. They wanted their son home, in America.

They wanted him to finish his education and pick up his 'real' life here. Osrik, naturally, wanted to please his wife's parents. And Brian was...spoiled. Hotheaded. There were a couple of incidents. He seduced and abandoned a serving girl. When the girl became pregnant, Osrik arranged a marriage for her with a steady, hardworking farmer. Also, Brian beat one of the grooms in the stables almost to death for putting his favorite horse away wet. Osrik wanted to send him to the Mystics then, the wise men beyond the Black Mountains. In Gullandria, troubled young people are often packed off to the Mystics, where they're taught a little discipline and made to understand the error of their ways.

"Brian refused to go, of course. And I interceded for him, to see he wasn't sent away. Brian was...a troublemaker. I see that now, from the perspective of many years. He had a cruel and selfish little heart."

"But back then?"

Ingrid lifted one shoulder in a regretful shrug. "I was used to loving him unconditionally. He was the 'baby' of our family. It was a huge blind spot with me. I wanted him to have what he wanted: citizenship and the title of prince. And Osrik kept putting him off. I was torn, I guess you could say—my beloved baby brother on one side, my parents and husband on the other. Finally Brian demanded the right to earn his place as a Gullandrian prince if Osrik wouldn't simply grant it to him. You see, in Gullandria—"

Liv smiled. "Mom. I know." Ingrid had explained it all, years ago, in her stories to her girls of the land of their birth. If a man or a woman of another country desired Gullandrian citizenship, he or she could take a Gullandrian spouse, or petition the king for a special quest—an assignment that, when accomplished, would earn the petitioner all rights as a true Gullandrian. "Why didn't Brian just find a Gullandrian girl and marry her? What about the servant he—"

Ingrid made a low sound in her throat. "My brother, marry a servant, a mere freewoman? Never. Didn't I mention he was a terrible snob?"

"My uncle sounds like a complete rat, and if not the serving girl, what about some lady or other? He *was* heir to a few Freyasdahl millions, right? And he was also the brother-in-law of the king. Even if he was ugly as a gnome and a total jerk on top of it, that should have made him attractive enough to some ambitious lady with the proper pedigree."

"Brian didn't want to do it that way. As time went by, he became nothing short of obsessed with the idea of 'earning' his citizenship by way of a special quest. Usually, in the past century or so, when the king grants a quest, it's something pretty mundane—to paint a public building or clean up a roadway. That, along with a routine course in citizenship and proof that a man has a means of supporting himself, is usually all it takes. But Brian wanted something dangerous, something exciting. And blinded to his faults as I was, that seemed to me a noble thing, a proof that he was a better man than everyone else thought him to be."

Liv knew what came next. "So Father finally gave your brother what he wanted."

Ingrid nodded. "It was a covert mission into the Black Mountains and on to the Vildelund, to bring back a certain high jarl lady who'd run off to join the *kvina soldars*. The lady never did return. I understand she became a fine warrior. My brother was found dead at the gateway to the mountains, his head severed from his body and left on a pike a mile farther on—and a mile beyond that, his male parts were tied so they dangled from the branches of a spruce tree."

Liv winced. "That's bad."

"Yes, it was."

"And you blamed Father."

"Not at first. First, I demanded that he muster all his military forces and send them marching to the Vildelund, to avenge Brian's death. He refused. He said that Brian was hated by many and there was no way to be certain who—or what—had killed him. Also, there was the fact that his body had been so horribly mutilated. In Gullandria, they only do things like that to the corpses of rapists or child molesters. Osrik said Brian must have deserved what he got. Osrik told me he wouldn't wage war on his own people to avenge the death of a cruel, spoiled fool— and after that, yes. I hated him. You girls were born and I never returned to our marriage bed. I insisted I was leaving him. At first, he said he would never let me go. But then I swore I'd divorce him. It was, after all, my right as a Gullandrian woman. He kept me captive in Tarngalla for a while. Eventually, when he couldn't stand the shame of being known as the king who had to keep his wife under lock and key to make her stay with him, we struck a bargain. I got you girls and the freedom to live in America.

He kept our sons to bring up as candidates for the throne when the Kingmaking came around again.''

Liv reached across the table once more. Her mother's hand clasped hers.

Ingrid went on, ''At the time, I was wild with grief—and guilt, too, I realize now. I even imagined Osrik had *wanted* Brian dead. That he'd as good as killed him, to send him on that hopeless mission. When at last he allowed me and you three girls to leave for California, I swore never again to set foot on Gullandrian soil.''

Liv asked softly, ''And now?''

Still holding tight to Liv's hand, Ingrid pushed back her chair and rose. She came around the table and stood over her daughter. ''Now, I would like once more, however briefly, to hold my eldest daughter in my arms.''

''Oh, Mom...'' Liv surged upward into Ingrid's embrace. Over her mother's shoulder, Liv sent Hildy a quivery smile.

After a minute, Ingrid took Liv by the arms and held her away enough to look into her eyes. ''It doesn't matter what vows I make now. Now, as the mother of three proud and beautiful daughters, I only ask the gods most humbly that the three Norns of destiny show my girls the way on the twisting roads of their own separate fates.''

The rattling fifty-seater Liv took from Heathrow arrived in Gullandria at three the following afternoon. It was a clear, cool day, with a brisk wind that made the rotors of the windmills lining the road to

Isenhalla spin so fast they seemed like ghostly circles, rippling against the sky.

There had been a black car waiting for her at the airport—sent by her father. She didn't ask Kaarin Karlsmon, who'd been assigned the job of escorting her, how her father knew that she was arriving. It suited her just fine that he knew she was there.

At the palace, Kaarin led Liv to the same rooms she'd shared with Brit during her previous visit. Brit was there, waiting, arms outstretched. Liv freshened up a little and changed into her favorite all-business dove-gray silk suit.

Brit hugged her again. "Knock 'im dead," she whispered.

"Oh, don't I wish."

Kaarin was ready and waiting in the suite's formal sitting room. "This way, Your Highness." She turned for the exit to the hallway.

Kaarin left her when they reached the tall doors. The guards pulled them wide. Liv's pulse picked up speed as she crossed the stone floor of the antechamber.

Her father was alone, seated behind his massive inlaid desk. He looked up as she entered.

"Well," he said. "It's about time."

She'd had a thousand trenchant, scathing points to make. She'd planned to descend on him, eloquent in her righteous fury, to bend him to her will—and to doing the right thing—by the sheer force and brilliance of her arguments.

But instead, she discovered, she had nothing to say to him beyond, "I'd like to speak with Finn, please. Will you have someone take me to him?"

Chapter Fourteen

The cell was of lusterless gray stone—all of it: walls, ceiling and floor. One small barred window, high up, let in a square of light and meted out a view of a tiny slice of Gullandrian sky. A rough stone fireplace contained the usual Gullandrian-style insert that meant it burned natural gas. At least, Liv thought, as cheerless as the accommodations were, he wouldn't be cold.

An arch in the wall perpendicular to the entry door led into shadow—a sleeping alcove, Liv assumed, maybe some rudimentary sort of bathroom. The furniture was the basics only: a rough table and two straight chairs. A recessed and grated ceiling fixture directly over the table cast a weak glow on an area perhaps four feet square, so that the corners of the room faded out into gray gloom. On the table lay a stack of books, a tablet, a few pens....

"Give a call through there, Highness, when you're ready to leave." The guard gestured at the small barred grate in the top of the heavy door.

Liv quelled a shiver. "Thank you. I will."

The man saluted and backed out, pulling the door shut as he went. Liv faced the room again and heard the key turn in the lock behind her.

Finn's voice came to her out of the darkness of the second room. "You shouldn't have come."

Liv swallowed away the traitorous tightness in her throat, faced the dark arch and announced, "Well, great to see you, too—that is, if I *could* see you."

He took form beneath the arch as he moved into the meager light. Her heart leaped and then seemed to stop cold in her chest. He was unshaven, his white silk shirt wrinkled and half-unbuttoned, his slacks unpressed. His eyes seemed so deep—and lightless. There were dark circles beneath them.

How could this have happened? How could her lighthearted playboy prince have been brought so low?

She wanted only to run to him, to throw her arms around him, pull his tousled head down and press her lips to his. But something in his haggard face stopped her. Something in those lightless eyes warned her to keep back.

"Why?" she asked simply.

For that she got a rueful shrug.

"Please, Finn. Tell me. Why has my father sent you here?"

He tipped his head, looked at her sideways. "You haven't talked to him?"

"I saw him for a minute or two, just long enough to ask that he take me to you."

Finn stepped closer and her heart seemed to swell with longing, to outgrow the space inside her chest. But he didn't reach for her. He grabbed one of the crude straight chairs, pulled it out and dropped into it. "Go back home. Forget about me. Your father is a good man, a reasonable man at heart. In time, he'll see the futility of keeping me here. I'll be released—a little ragged, somewhat unclean, but not appreciably the worse for wear."

She took a step closer. "You didn't answer my question. Why are you here?"

"Go home."

"It's something to do with me, isn't it?"

He rested one fine hand on the table, idly flipped open the cover of a book, then sharply flicked it closed again. "Go home."

She took the second step that brought her to the table and then she pulled out the other chair and sat opposite him. "There's no sense in refusing to tell me. You'll only force me to ask *him*. I have a feeling he's going to be all too willing to explain to me exactly why he's put you here."

Finn grabbed the book and hurled it across the room. It landed against the stone with a hard smack, then slid, pages ruffling, to the floor.

Liv looked at him for a long, cool moment. Then she rose, picked up the book and carried it back to the table, where she placed it on top of the stack. "Talk to me. Please."

A stare-down ensued, a strange echo of their earlier times together—only reversed. Now he was the one scowling and angry, and she returned his glare with a calm, pleasant smile.

"Please," she said at last, softly. Tenderly.

"Go home." He stood. And then he turned and walked away from her, disappearing again into the darkness beyond the archway.

Her father rose from the chair behind his big inlaid desk when Liv returned to his private audience chamber. Prince Medwyn, his Grand Counselor, stood behind him, to his right.

"Well," said Osrik. "Have you enjoyed a warm and tender reunion with the father of my grandchild?"

Liv resisted the urge to say something a woman should never say to a king, even if that king happened to be her father. "He won't tell me why you sent him there."

Osrik shook his head. "So stubborn. And so surprising. Prince Finn has, until very recently, ever been a reasonable man."

"So I'm guessing you'll tell me. Why did you send him there?"

Her father sank to his chair again. He laid both hands on the desktop and looked down at them. He appeared to be studying the big ruby on his right hand. He lifted his proud gray head and looked at Liv once more. "He tells me you refuse to marry him."

Liv resisted the urge to explain herself. Instead, she proudly drew her shoulders back and answered, "That's correct."

A slow smile took form on Osrik's still-handsome

face. ''Well, then. You have it in your power to secure his immediate release.''

She sucked in a slow breath. ''By marrying him.''

''Ah. Good girl. Bright girl.''

Liv felt her temper rise. She made an effort to speak in an even tone. ''I don't believe this. You threw a man prison because he couldn't convince me to marry him.''

Her father gestured broadly. ''Ahem. Well. More or less.''

Clearly there was more going on here than she knew, more than she *wanted* to know. ''What more?'' she asked bleakly.

''It matters not.''

''Not to *you,* maybe.''

''The plain fact is, you refused to marry him, in spite of all his efforts to seduce and cajole you. His charms are legendary, yet they failed against your stubborn determination to bear your child in shame. I was…disappointed in him. Extremely so. I sent him to Tarngalla in order that he might have the leisure to ponder my displeasure.''

''This is not the whole story, Father. I know there's more to it.''

Osrik sighed. ''You *are* here, now, aren't you? You've left the summer employment you value so highly and come all this way to aid him. From this I deduce that the father of your child must mean *something* to you.''

''Of course he does.'' More than she had understood until she'd seen him in the darkness, brought so low. More than she wanted her father to know.

More, she realized, than she quite knew how to handle.

A rueful gleam lit the king's dark eyes. "Medwyn and I have been talking," he said. "At length. I see no harm in revealing to you now that at one time, we hoped that Elli, or you, or perhaps even Brit might marry Medwyn's son, Eric. Eric is a fine man, much beloved by the people, a good candidate for king when the time for the Kingmaking is on us again. Since your brothers are gone, I have dared to dream that someday my grandson, at least, will claim the throne.

"However, things are not working out quite as I had planned. Elli has married my warrior. Eric has disappeared into the Vildelund and refuses, at least up to this point, to return. You are with child by Finn. Much discussion has led us to understand that we must be more...open to other ways of viewing this situation."

None of this information was particularly surprising to Liv. Now that his sons were gone, it was only logical that her father would want one of his daughters to marry the future king.

Osrik continued. "As a Danelaw, Finn is very much eligible for kingship. He could be groomed toward that end. Were you to marry him, you would be queen. And he seems an open-minded sort of man at heart, a man who would be quite amenable to the suggestions of a brilliant, politically minded wife. You could be, in the truest sense, the power behind the throne."

Liv gaped at her father.

"Close your mouth, daughter," said Osrik. "And tell us what you think of our idea."

Liv shook her head. "Oh, Father. You just don't get it."

Osrik looked weary suddenly. "What is it I don't 'get'?"

"I don't want to be queen. I could never be satisfied with being the power *behind* anything."

Her father almost smiled. "Ah. Such ambition."

"That's right. I'm ambitious, and proud of it."

"But do you have any hope of ever realizing your ambition?"

"Yes. I believe I do. I'll be a senator, or maybe governor."

Osrik grunted. "I know they're...progressive in America. But isn't it still the norm for a woman to marry first and *then* have children?"

Liv stood tall. "Times change."

Father and daughter regarded each other across the expanse of his desk. Osrik said, "Marry Finn. Set him free. And give your child a name."

"And if I don't?"

"You can consider yourself responsible for his extended imprisonment."

The three princesses met in the private sitting room of the suite assigned to Liv and Brit. Brit assured them they could speak freely. She'd made an ally of one of the agents at the National Investigative Bureau—the Gullandrian version of the FBI. The agent had dropped in for a visit just yesterday and swept the rooms for bugs. And Brit had sent the cook and the maid out on a few errands, a series of odd jobs that should take them several hours.

Brit said, "This is how I see it. Dad wanted Finn to get you to marry him—any way he had to. Finn drew the line at force. And it's off to Tarngalla for him."

Elli was nodding. "I buy that. After all, when Father decided he wanted *me* here in Gullandria, he sent Hauk to kidnap me."

Liv gave her middle sister a look of pure disbelief. "You never told me that."

Elli waved a hand. "It all worked out, didn't it? And the kidnapping part only lasted for a few hours. Then I realized I *wanted* to come. We reached an agreement. From then on, Hauk was merely my escort."

"I don't know if I like the way you say 'escort.'"

Elli sighed. "Livvy, it's in the past. Let it go."

"But—" Liv cut herself off as she saw the impatient expressions on the faces of both of her sisters. "Okay, okay. So you're saying Father wanted Finn to...abduct me? To somehow force me to marry him?" Both of her sisters were nodding. "Oh, come on. People don't *do* things like that anymore. It's barbaric."

"By our standards, maybe," Elli said. "But to a Gullandrian, your refusal to marry the father of your child is heartless in the extreme, a barbarism far beyond mere kidnapping."

Liv stared at Elli. "You almost sound as if you feel the same way."

Elli's blue eyes were so sad. "If you only knew what Hauk lived through as a child—what it was like for him, the ugly names they called him, the ostracism he suffered, simply because his mother refused to marry his father.''

Liv swallowed. ''Really bad, huh?''

''Terrible. There was plenty of physical abuse, of course. Many of the other children felt it was one-hundred-percent okay to do everything from throwing rocks at him, to ganging up on him and beating him bloody. But he says getting beat up was by no means the worst of it—and neither was the frequent name-calling. The worst was the constant awareness that he was not and never would be the equal of any other person born of married parents, no matter how low, mean or stupid those legitimate kids might be. He was a fitz and as a fitz, he was a rung or two down the ladder from a true human being.''

''That's hideous,'' said Liv.

''Yes,'' said Elli, ''it is.''

Both of her sisters were watching her expectantly. Liv looked from one to the other. ''You both think I should do it, that I should marry Finn.''

Brit didn't even hesitate. ''Under the circumstances, absolutely.'' Elli showed her support with a quick, firm nod. Brit went on, ''Look. Even if you don't think the marriage will last, you're nuts for the guy. I can see it in your eyes every time you say his name. It's not as if there's anyone else you're in love with or anything. And if it doesn't work out, well, you stay married at least until the baby is born and then you go your separate ways. Divorce is never a great option for anyone. But in your situation, I'd say the possibility of it isn't near as awful as leaving Finn to rot in Tarngalla.''

Elli was sitting forward, eager to make a point or two of her own. "And you *are* of Gullandrian descent. Your father is king here."

Brit chimed in, indicating Elli, "Your sister lives here."

Elli continued. "You might want to visit again, now and then. If you don't marry Finn, I guarantee you'll never want to bring your child here. From what Hauk has told me, things *are* changing. Being a fitz isn't as bad as it used be. But it's bad enough. Even today, it would be an act of callous cruelty to bring your illegitimate child here, to put a little one through the intolerance he'd have to endure if you did."

The scary thing was, Liv found she agreed with them. "You two make it seem as if there's no other choice."

Brit said, "Hey. If you see some other option we haven't thought of—please. Share."

Liv had nothing to share. Her father had done what he'd set out to do. She was boxed in tight. The only way out was to become Finn's wife.

Liv spoke with her father first thing the next morning. An hour later, she went to see Finn.

He was sitting at the table in the front room of his cell when the guard ushered her in. He closed the book in front of him and leaned back in his chair, head tipped to the side, regarding her with an expression both distant and assessing.

Her heart raced and her palms felt damp with nervousness. And also with longing. She'd been pondering, through the sleepless night just past, how very much she'd missed him in the days since he'd left her in California. Somehow, seeing him again yesterday had brought it sharply home to her. She wanted his arms around her. She wanted him back the way he'd always been before, charming and brilliant, flirting relentlessly and making the teasing fun of male-female interaction seem like high art. She wanted to see the gleam in those amber eyes again, the old gleam of humor and heat.

Now, as she looked close, she saw that his eyes did gleam. But it wasn't the same. Now it was...dangerous. Feral. Those eyes warned her away even as her own longing pulled her on.

Behind her, the key turned in the lock. The guard's trudging footsteps moved away from the thick door. "Well," she said, her voice so bright it verged on brittle, "you look much better."

"Yes." He sketched an elegant shrug. "Not an hour ago, they led me to the showers and presented me with a change of clothes. And now, here I am, all cleaned up, at Her Royal Highness's pleasure." Somehow he made getting cleaned up for her sound reprehensible.

"Oh, Finn. Why are you so...angry with me? I did come all this way. I'm *here*. I'll do whatever I can for you."

He remained unmoved. "What you can do for me is to go home. I thought I made that clear when we spoke yesterday."

She dared to step closer, to reach for the other chair. "Do you mind? May I sit down?"

His gaze moved over her, burning where it touched. "Is there some way I can stop you?"

"I'll take that as rhetorical." She forced a smile, pulled out the chair and sat.

Finn watched her. She hadn't a clue what he was thinking. He seemed to be seething as he slouched in his chair and looked her up and down. At the same time, there was something frankly sexual in the way he stared at her. As if he wanted her desperately and despised himself for it. As if he couldn't decide whether to order her out again or grab her and carry her into the darkness beyond the arch on the side wall.

A hot shiver ran through her. She wished he would do it—grab her, make love to her. She missed his touch so very much. And if he was cruel, so what? She could take it.

She could take anything, if only she could somehow break through this awful, angry wall of silence between them.

He spoke, too softly. "You have something to say to me?"

She gulped. "Yes. I've talked with my father."

"Ah."

"He won't back down. Marry me, and you're a free man. Otherwise, you might never get out of here."

He waved a hand lazily, the movement in direct contradiction to the focused intent in his eyes. "He'll change his mind. Once you go back to America, he'll have to admit that it accomplishes nothing to keep me here."

"I think you're wrong."

"It doesn't matter what you think."

"It does if I'm right. I'd bet you ten years' income

from my trust fund that if I don't marry you, you'll be here for a very long time.''

One side of his beautiful mouth lifted in a joyless approximation of a smile and he indicated the stack of books and the tablet and pens on the table in front of him. ''I'll catch up on my reading. Work on my memoirs. And besides, it's not as if I have anything all that important to do, anyway.''

''Oh, please. What about your investments? Don't you have to manage them?''

''Don't concern yourself.''

''But I do concern myself.'' For that, she got another shrug. She tried again. ''And what about your sister and your grandfather? They must be worried sick about you.''

''They'll manage. They always have.''

Oh, she would never make him see reason on this. She said it straight out. ''Please. Won't you marry me?''

''No.''

Liv shut her eyes and counted to ten.

Then she tried again. ''Finn, I've thought it over. I've decided I was wrong before. And you were right. Marriage is the best way, for us. For our baby. I regret that I told you no so many times. I hope you can forgive me for that. But I want to marry you now. I truly do.''

He chuckled, the sound without humor. ''Very touching. And also a lie.''

She sat forward and let her urgency show. ''No. It's not a lie. It's the only way. Please. Won't you do it? Won't you be my husband?''

He neither moved nor spoke. The bleak room seemed to echo with emptiness.

She rushed to fill it. "I've talked it over at length with my infuriating father *and* with my sisters. I've...reevaluated the whole situation."

"Have you?" He spoke coolly, distantly.

"Oh, Finn. Why won't you admit it? Whatever you say to the contrary, you and I both know that you're not getting out of here any time soon—not unless you marry me."

"So be it."

She glared at him for several seconds. It had zero effect. He gazed back at her steadily, his face a blank.

It wasn't easy, but somehow she managed *not* to start shouting at him. She asked with measured care, "How am I going to get through to you?"

"You're not. Go home."

It was too much. She threw her head back and let out a shriek of pure frustration at his pointless pigheadedness. "Oh, this is ridiculous." She jumped to her feet and rounded on him. "Even if you've decided for some reason to play it disgustingly noble and rot away in here for years, the least you can do is think of the baby. You know it's not fair to the baby. He—or she—will be Gullandrian every bit as much as he'll be an American. If we aren't married when he's born, he'll be an outcast in his father's land. I can't do that, to my baby, to *our* baby. It just isn't right."

For a moment, she was certain he was going to rise and walk away, to disappear into the dim alcove beyond the arch again and leave her standing there wondering what to do now. But then he spoke. "I thought you said it didn't matter, that he would be American and in America, children are raised all the time by—''

She didn't let him finish. "I know what I said. And I realize now I was wrong."

"No." He shook his head slowly, his gaze on the cold gray stone floor. "You were right. I'm sure the baby will do well whether his parents are married or not—in America."

She sat and leaned forward, straining toward him, wishing he would lift his head, meet her eyes. "But not here. Here, he'd be an outcast."

"That didn't seem to matter much to you before."

"At the time we spoke of it, I didn't really even believe I was pregnant. Now that I've had a few days to think about it, now I've accepted in my heart that I really am having a baby, I see things in a different light. Oh, Finn, if we don't marry, it's not going to be…viable to let the baby come here. Do you want that, really? Do you want your child never to know that precious Balmarran of yours? Never to see the land of his father's birth?"

He lifted his head at last. His gaze probed hers. "I never wanted that. But you've been so…unyielding. So determined that the baby would be born American, that his status here would never matter, as he was never coming here."

"I was wrong. I know that now. What more can I say except *please?* Will you marry me? Will you give our child his father's name?"

He stared at her for a long time. "You're certain? It's what you want?"

"I am. It is."

"To marry me."

She nodded.

He asked, "And then?" She glanced away. He knew her answer and said it for her. "You'll go back to America."

"You could...come with me."

His gaze caught hers, held it. "You could stay here, for a while—come with me, see Balmarran..."

She shook her head. In the end, he had his life and she had hers. It wasn't going to be a marriage in the usual sense of the word. "Finn, I'm sorry. I have my internship to finish. I can't afford much more time away, or I'll have to sacrifice the units. And then there's the fall semester coming up...."

For the first time, his eyes softened. "It's all right. I understand. You have your ambitions. And I want you to have them."

Her heart broke a little then, because she believed him. He didn't want to take her dreams away. She bit back the tears and whispered, "Thank you."

He reached across then, at last. "When?"

She put her hand in his, glorying at the warmth as his fingers closed around hers. "Friday," she said. Gullandrians, if possible, always married on Friday, as Friday was Frigg's day and Frigg was the goddess of hearth and home.

Finn nodded. "It is fitting. On Friday, then."

Chapter Fifteen

The wedding was a simple affair. The guest list for the exchange of vows could be counted on two hands: the bride's sisters and their father, the king; Hauk and Medwyn; Eveline and Balder Danelaw.

In the Viking way, the short ceremony took place outside, in the parkland below the palace. Liv wore a simple long pale blue dress and a traditional bridal crown woven of straw and wheat and garlanded with flowers. She and Finn exchanged swords as Viking custom decreed and then, on the ends of those swords, they traded rings. Following the Viking ceremony, a Lutheran minister presided over a swift exchange of Christian vows.

With both sets of vows behind them, the small wedding party retired to the palace where a feast had been set out and more guests—princes and ladies currently in residence—joined the celebration. There were the rituals of strength and of fertility and a shared first loving cup of ale. There was dancing and a series of poetic recitations by two of Gullandria's most prominent skalds.

Liv made a special point, as the evening progressed, to steal a few private moments with Finn's grandfather and then with his sister. The conversation with Balder went quite well, she thought. He was a large, gentle man with a surprisingly full head of white hair and a trim gray beard. He enfolded her in a bear hug and whispered in a gruff voice, "Welcome to our family."

Eveline was another story. A beauty with long black hair and flashing blue eyes, her full mouth was set in a rebellious scowl.

"Grandfather's a softhearted fool," Finn's sister announced when Liv came and stood by her and tried to share a few civil sentences. "But not me. I know His Majesty threw Finn into Tarngalla and I know it was your fault. And as soon as you marry him, you're leaving him, going back to America. What kind of a marriage is that, anyway, if you live there and he lives here?"

Liv hardly knew where to begin. "Eveline, I'm sorry you're upset, but really, what Finn and I will do with our lives is between the two of us."

"You're sorry?" The girl made a small, disgusted noise in her throat. "I don't believe that. You're going and he's staying and that makes no sense at all. He tries to pretend it's all perfectly fine with him, but I know my own brother. It's not fine. He's not happy, and he always *used* to be happy. What did you *do* to him?''

That one caught Liv completely off guard. ''Nothing. I didn't—''

''Oh, you needn't lie to me. I see right through you. And I don't like what I see. Soon I'll be off to train with the *kvina soldars*. Maybe I'll come looking for you in America someday.''

Liv had collected herself by then. She asked coolly, ''Now, why does that sound like a warning?''

''Because when I find you, I'll cut your heart out and eat it raw.''

Nothing would be gained, Liv reminded herself, if she grabbed this little witch around her pretty neck and squeezed until her manners improved. And Finn was coming toward them from across the room. ''Here comes your brother now. Maybe you'd like to tell him about your grisly plans for me.''

Eveline stuck out her chin and yanked her shoulders back. ''Tell him yourself.''

Liv leaned toward the girl and spoke for her ears alone. ''I think not. I think this is his wedding day and a loving sister wouldn't ruin it by making an ugly scene.''

Eveline pursed up her pretty mouth all the tighter. ''I'm not saying a word.'' She turned and waited for her brother.

Finn closed in on them, grinning. ''My two favorite women in all the world.'' He put his arm around his sister. ''Having a good time, Evie?''

''Wonderful.'' She slid him a sullen look.

He shot a rueful glance Liv's way. ''Isn't she a charmer?''

"Oh, absolutely."

He gave his sister's shoulder an affectionate squeeze and reached for his bride. "Come. Dance with me."

Liv went into his arms, thinking with a stab of mingled joy and regret how very good it felt to be there. Too soon, she'd be thousands of miles away from him. He whirled her off across the floor and Eveline slipped from her line of sight. When again she had a clear view of the place where she'd stood with his sister, the black-haired beauty was gone.

At midnight, Elli and Brit and several of the younger ladies in attendance led Liv upstairs. They took her to the large, beautifully appointed suite where she'd been installed earlier that day.

The four-poster bed in the master bedroom was wide and deep, covered in shimmering layers of white silk, the mahogany posts turned to look like coiling dragon tails, with intricately carved dragon-head finials crowning each one.

The women helped her to change to a white silk nightgown and then put her in the bed. The men brought Finn up soon after.

Liv remembered the laughter and bawdy exchanges when Elli and Hauk were bedded only three weeks before. This was a much more subdued proceeding, everything quieter, more sedate. Maybe it was the hasty nature of the wedding, maybe everyone knew that this union was one of necessity rather than one of true choice and thus they behaved more seriously, not that it really mattered to Liv. She liked it this way, minus the suggestive remarks and silly sexual banter. Within minutes, the men and the ladies were bowing from the room, leaving Finn fully dressed and standing near the door.

In the quiet, bride and groom regarded each other. Liv's heart was racing and her skin felt too warm. She put her hands against her cheeks.

Finn frowned. "Are you ill?"

She shook her head. "It's crazy, but I'm so nervous. You'd think we'd never done this before."

Finn smiled—a slow, very sexy smile. It was almost the same smile he used to bestow so easily. The only difference was the distinct note of sadness in it.

She thought of his sister's words. *He's not happy. He always used to be happy. What did you do to him?*

"Oh, Finn. Are you all right?"

He winked. "Exceedingly so."

Beside him stood a shield-backed chair. He dropped to the damask seat and removed his soft black boots. Then he stood and shrugged out of his velvet wedding coat. The fine ruffled shirt came next. He tossed both on the chair.

Liv's breath got stuck in her chest. He was truly a beautiful man, so lean and strong, the muscles of his arms and shoulders sharply defined, his chest broad and deep, tapering to a tight, hard waist. And then there was that wonderful silky trail of hair that ran down the center of his torso, pointing the way to the delights below.

"Why do you smile?" he asked.

"Because you are so very gorgeous."

He looked at her sideways. "As are you—though the blankets obscure the view."

Liv lifted the covers and tossed them aside. Then she dropped back to the pile of soft pillows and wiggled her toes. "Better?"

"You have the *most* attractive toes."

"Why, thank you, sir."

His gaze caressed her, from those wriggling toes all the way up to her blushing face. "The gown is lovely. It clings in a most provocative manner." There was such heat in those amber eyes. Heat and knowing and humor...and tenderness.

The truth she already knew came suddenly poignantly clear: Tonight was their first night as man and wife and also, essentially, their last.

She would leave for America tomorrow. Perhaps, in the future, there would be passionate reunions. After all, she couldn't get enough of his touch and he seemed to feel the same about her. Such heat would not fade swiftly. It could burn on for years, this fire between them, rekindled whenever they met again, which, given the baby she carried, would be bound to happen now and then.

She stared into his gleaming eyes. Yes. Such heat...

But it couldn't last.

And it would never grow deeper.

For a true bond to develop, they would need time. They would need a daily striving together toward shared goals.

With a continent and an ocean between them, what might have been would never have a chance to happen, let alone to grow.

And eventually, untended, the fire between them would fade.

Strange that she would think of this now, that she'd find herself missing what she hadn't even really considered before—a life with Finn, as his wife.

He asked quietly, "What has happened to your smile?"

Liv ordered the sadness away. They did have tonight. And she *would* make the most of it. "Why don't you...come closer?"

He didn't move, only murmured, "From sadness to siren, in the blink of an eye."

"Oh, Finn. Please." She held out her arms. "Won't you come here?"

Still he held his ground, but the gleam in his eyes said much. In a low voice, he suggested, "Take off the gown."

From her nest of pillows, she looked down the length of her body at the gown in question, then up at him, one eyebrow lifted.

He chuckled. "Yes. That one."

She slid her hands to her hips and took the fabric in either fist. Slowly she began to gather it up. He watched her.

And she watched him.

She felt the silky slide of the cloth whispering upward, over her shins, her knees, the length of her thighs.

"Stop," he whispered, when the gown lay across her hipbones and the soft curls between her legs were revealed to him. He started for her.

She let go of the gown and reached for him.

It was very late, nearly morning. The heavy curtains were drawn across the jewel-paned windows, letting in only a sliver of twilit glow from outside.

Liv woke with a sigh and for a moment wondered where she was. Then she remembered. She slid her hand over to Finn's side of the bed. Nothing.

She sat up. "Finn?"

He appeared from the shadows, a denser darkness within the gloom.

"Where were you?"

"Right here. Sitting. Watching."

"Watching me?" He made a low noise. She knew it for a yes. "Is something wrong?"

"Not a thing."

She didn't believe him, but he gave her no chance to argue the point. He caught the edge of the blanket and tore it back. His gaze swept over her, burning where it touched.

His eyes had that predatory, feral look in them, the look she'd first seen in his gray prison cell. She stared back at him, unafraid. Slowly she held out her arms.

With a low, hungry sound, he came down to her, clutching for her.

She enfolded him, wrapping her legs around him, accepting eagerly his first hard, deep thrust, crying out again as the thrusts continued, a glorious volley of them. She met each one.

Seated within her, he stilled. His head was tucked into the curve of her shoulder, his arms banded tight around her, stealing her breath, crushing her ribs. He thrust hard again with a guttural moan.

She was moaning, too, at the feel of him so deep

inside her. His arms loosened just enough that she could breathe again. She sighed in relief.

He rose up on his elbows. She met his eyes.

Below, he began to move once more. She moved with him—a liquid dance of heat and need. The pleasure was so exquisite, so intense, she could only just bear it.

And then it became too much. She let her eyelids droop shut and tossed her head on the pillow.

"No." The command seemed dragged up from far down inside him. He captured her face between his hands and held it still until she looked at him again.

"What?" she cried. "Yes. Anything…"

But he said nothing, only continued to look at her as he moved within her, until she thought she might go mad with the sheer erotic agony of it.

She was…

Sea grass on the ocean floor. The sun would never reach her. Blind and swaying in the velvet darkness, only the deepest and most powerful currents moved her, caressed her.…

She was a white bird flying into a summer storm. The warm, hard rain was in her eyes, slicking along her feathers. Lightning flashed too close, brightness flaring all around her. Thunder rolled away through the dark sky.

She was a waterfall—a waterfall in a secret rain forest, tumbling hard and joyfully over mossy rocks, white spume glistening, falling.

Falling…

He thrust in so hard. She surged up, closing tight around him. All of her—arms, legs, *everything,* holding him, claiming him, as the pulsing of their mutual release began.

Chapter Sixteen

Her flight left at quarter past noon. Finn, freshly showered and dressed in a casual shirt and dark slacks, sat in the shield-backed chair and watched her gather her things.

"You don't need to rush. And you don't need to put up with the inconvenience of commercial flights. Your father would gladly give you the use of one of his jets."

She finished folding the shirt she had in her hands and tucked it carefully into the open suitcase. She didn't want to cancel her flight, to ask her father to provide transportation for her. She didn't feel up to dealing with him and she was afraid to linger. Every moment she stayed only made her want to stay longer.

"I've got my flights all arranged. I'd just as soon go ahead with what I've planned."

What she planned was to leave immediately. She should have been ready hours ago, really. But Finn was too tempting. They'd stayed in bed too long. She had no time now—not to see her father, not to kiss her sisters goodbye. Phone calls later, from stateside, would have to do.

Finn seemed to have no more to say. The big room seemed far too quiet as she finished her packing— quiet and somehow shadowed, though the bright light of a clear day shone in the windows.

It didn't take long. She zipped both suitcases shut and engaged the combination locks. "There."

He stood. "All right, then."

"You don't have to—"

He put up a hand. "Don't say it." He took the larger of the two bags. "Let's go."

At the airport, Finn had the driver take the car right out onto the tarmac. Airport security saw who they were and waved them ahead to where the small commuter plane was waiting with the boarding stairs down and the passengers filing on.

Finn caught her arm when she reached for the door handle. "We have a moment. The driver will see to your luggage."

The man behind the wheel got out and went around to the trunk.

Finn pulled her to him. His mouth hovered above hers, his breath sweet and hot on her face. "Viking tradition calls for a morning gift—a man gives his wife the keys to all his houses and holdings. A Viking's wife will need the keys—Viking men, after all, are prone to row off in their dragon-prowed ships and not return for months at a time.''

She ached all over at the reality of leaving him. ''Just kiss me. Please...''

He obliged her, his mouth hard at first and demanding, and then softening, turning gentle, his tongue delving in.

He ended it too soon. ''I suppose there's no point in giving you the keys to a castle you will never see.''

She looked at his eyes and his mouth, at the fine, strong line of his jaw. Not to touch him could not be borne. She laid a hand against his cheek. ''Oh, Finn.''

''Stay.'' His breath came ragged, as if he'd run a hard race.

''I can't. Come with me.''

He pulled back. ''Why?''

''Because I can't bear for you not to.''

He looked at her for a long time. And then he shook his head. ''Here.'' He held out a white box, perhaps four inches square. The box was tied with a midnight-blue satin ribbon. ''I never did find the moment to give you this.'' He put the box in her hand. ''Open it later, when you're safely home. And now, kiss me once more.''

She lifted her mouth and for one last, shining, too-brief span of time felt herself melting into him.

And then he reached behind her and pushed open her door. ''Go. Now.''

She turned quickly and slid out onto the pavement, standing tall on shaky legs, a cool, sea-scented wind blowing against her face. She whirled for the plane and didn't look back in spite of the small knot of reporters shouting her name behind her. She *couldn't* look back.

If she did, she knew she would throw over everything she'd ever dreamed of to stay in Gullandria with the beautiful playboy prince who had somehow managed to steal away her heart.

There was a delay at Heathrow. Mechanical difficulties. A scheduling snafu. The excuse changed every time a longer wait was announced. The afternoon wore on into evening.

Finally Liv learned that the flight was canceled altogether. She shuffled from airline to airline, but she couldn't get a guaranteed flight until the next day.

She went on standby. A couple of intrepid reporters had appeared by then. They hovered several yards away, waiting, no doubt, for her to do something newsworthy. She got rid of them by granting a quick impromptu interview.

Yes, she and Finn *had* married. And she was utterly thrilled to be his bride. But her darling husband understood she had a summer job commitment; he himself had his duties at his estate in Gullandria. They were parting for a time, but they'd be together again soon.

It wasn't a lie, exactly. *Soon*, after all, could mean just about anything.

She gave them permission to snap few pictures and then, at last, they went away. She sat at the gate and she waited, watching the other standby passengers: the executive types with their pinched expressions, their laptops always open and their phones permanently glued to one ear. And the retired couples, holding hands, looking pleased with themselves, off to see the world in their waning years. And the harried mothers on vacation with their little ones—little ones who too quickly grew weary of Game Boys and picture books.

One woman had a baby—how old? Three or four months? Liv really didn't know. She'd never been one to hover over other people's infants, making silly cooing noises, declaring, ''Oh, what an angel—and how old is he?'' She left that kind of stuff to Elli, who was born to be a mother.

And the plain fact was, she didn't feel any more like cooing right then than she ever had. It was just another of those shocking moments when the truth she already knew decided to make itself painfully clear.

In nine months or so, she'd be like that woman, holding her baby in her arms, swaying gently back and forth, making small, soothing noises, looking down at the scrunched-up red face within the blankets, absurdly in love the way mothers always seemed to be with their newborns.

She thought of the birth then, of *giving* birth. Oh, God. She was going to be doing that. In nine months or so.

She put her hand over her flat stomach and wondered how the two of them were going to survive it.

They would. Of course they would. Women and their babies rarely died during labor anymore. The two of them were going to be fine.

But what about Finn? Okay, they didn't have the

kind of marriage that most people had. But now that she had let herself think of it, she definitely wanted him to be there. Really, he *had* to be there for the baby's birth. He had the right, as the baby's father, and besides, she truly couldn't bear the thought of going through all that difficulty and pain and sweaty unpleasantness without him.

She fumbled in her big shoulder bag, looking for her phone. Finn had given her a couple of numbers—to his cell and to the main line at Balmarran—in case she ever needed to reach him.

Well, what could be more important than a father's presence at a baby's birth? Nothing. Nothing at all. She found the phone and flipped it open and started to dial his cell number.

Halfway through, she stopped. She flipped the phone shut and let it drop to her lap.

She was being ridiculous and she knew it. There was no need to call Finn right this moment about something that wasn't going to happen for months yet.

It was only…

She missed him. Terribly.

A few hours away from him and all she wanted was to get back to him, to see his face, hear his voice, feel his touch.

Oh, this was bad. This was very, very bad.

She put the phone in her bag again and took out the little white box he'd given her. He'd said to open it when she got home. She should probably follow his instructions.

But she'd never been all that good at following instructions. She always had to make her own rules, do things her own way. He had to know that about her by now.

And really, how much could it matter if she opened it now or later?

She took the end of the bow and gave it a tug. The ribbon went loose. She pushed it out of the way and removed the lid and found...her blue satin panties. The ones she'd lost that fateful night.

Liv sat back, vaguely irritated. Really now. What kind of morning gift was that? She'd been hoping for something sweet and romantic.

A love poem.

Jewelry.

Jewelry, a man like Finn with all his amorous experience ought know, was never amiss as a gift for a lady.

But her own panties?

Uh-uh.

She lifted them by the elastic and held them high, scowling at them, not stopping to think that the travelers around her might find the sight of her dangling a pair of satin panties distinctly odd.

"Ahem." A white-haired lady in the seat opposite her coughed into her heavily veined, beringed hand.

Liv shoved the panties back into the box and replaced the lid.

Right then, the boarding call began for her prospective flight. Ten minutes later, all the confirmed passengers had filed through the doorway. They began calling the standbys. Hers was the third name on the list. Liv heard it and didn't move.

More names were called. Still Liv sat where she was.

Finally the attendant shut the door. Liv watched out the window as the plane taxied off toward the runway.

A long time went by. A whole new group of travelers surrounded her, more aging tourists and young families and busy type A's. Another plane landed. The doors were opened and the passengers spilled out.

They were just starting to board yet another flight when Liv rose and returned to the ticket counter. She bought a ticket for the next plane to Gullandria.

It would depart tomorrow at 9:45 a.m.

In a daze, she caught a shuttle and found herself deposited at the Crowne Plaza hotel. She checked in and went to her room and ordered room service. She ate sitting on the plaid bedspread, channel-surfing and wondering if she might have, just possibly, gone out of her mind.

Time after time, she picked up the phone and then set it down again. What was to say?

"I've gone insane. I'm throwing over my internship and coming to see you at your precious Balmarran."

Oh, it was impossible. What about her plans for her life? She really did have to be crazy, to be thinking what she was thinking.

In the end, she called her mother. Ingrid picked up on the third ring.

"Mom?"

"Livvy? Where are you? Are you—?"

"I'm in a hotel right outside London. And yes, I'm okay. I'm stark raving nuts, but I'm okay."

"The wedding? Did you—"

"Yes. I did it. I married Finn."

"Oh," said her mother. Liv could hear the tears in her voice. "I'm glad, I truly am, but I thought you were supposed to be on your way home now."

"I am. I was. But I couldn't do it. I'm going back."

"Oh, sweetheart."

"I just, well, I can't seem to leave, you know? I want to be with Finn."

"I know."

"It's so unlike me. Throwing my internship over, for a *man*."

Ingrid gave a low laugh. "Not just any man. He is, after all, your husband."

"I miss him," Liv said in a small voice. "I want to be with him. I want to...work things out with him."

"Of course you do."

"I think he's angry with me. Oh, Mom. I don't know *what's* wrong with him."

"I'm sure he's hurt."

"Why? What did I *do*? It's not as if he didn't know how I am. It's not as if I never told him that I had plans for my life and I—"

"Just go to him. Just work it through."

"His sister hates me. She's sure it's all my fault that he's so broody and mean lately, and you know, I think she's probably right. I think...he really loves me, Mom. And I think I love him."

"You'll work it out."

"You keep saying that."

"Because there's nothing else to say. Because I know that you will. I knew it the moment I met him.

The two of you are perfect for each other. You need a little humor and passion in your life. And I think that Finn needs a little direction.''

''You're sure? You don't think I'm crazy to be doing this?''

''I absolutely do not.''

''But what about—''

''There'll be other internships.''

''He wants to live *there,* in Gullandria. How will I—''

''One step at a time,'' her mother said.

''One step at a time,'' she told herself the next morning. ''I'm going to visit him at his castle. We'll see how it goes.…''

She called his cell phone as soon as she reached Gullandria, but he didn't answer. She left a brief message, then tried the number at Balmarran. The housekeeper picked up.

Prince Finn was not taking calls.

''But is he *there?*''

The housekeeper confirmed that, yes, the prince was at Balmarran.

''Then will you please tell him that his *wife* would like to speak with him?''

The housekeeper asked her if she would please hold.

''Yes. Yes, of course.'' Liv waited.

The next voice on the line was one she didn't especially want to hear. ''What do *you* want?'' Eveline demanded.

Liv suppressed a sigh. ''To speak to my husband.''

· "He doesn't wish to be disturbed." The line went dead.

Liv muttered a few rude words beneath her breath. Really, she should have strangled the girl when she had the chance.

She decided she'd give up on phoning him first. She would go to him, somehow get past the housekeeper and his overbearing brat of a sister, and speak to him face to face.

But first, she had to find out where Balmarran was. Most likely, her father would know.

Osrik started in on her the minute she entered the private chamber.

"Odin's bones, what is it now? I thought you were deserting your husband and returning to America as fast as public air transport could carry you."

"I changed my mind."

Her father sent her a wary look. "Should we be heartened? Is it possible you've come to your senses and realized your place is at your husband's side?"

"Sure, be heartened. Why not? And I think it's probably better for both of us if I don't even try to answer that second question. I understand Finn has returned to Balmarran."

"Yes, and with a dark look in his eye and a scowl on his too-handsome face. I never thought I'd see the day that Finn Danelaw couldn't spare a smile and a clever remark. But that day has come, and I'm shamed to say my own daughter has brought it upon us."

Liv resisted the urge to defend herself. She knew her father well enough by then to understand that arguing with him would accomplish zip, beyond possibly incurring the royal wrath.

She didn't need that. Between Finn and that sister of his, she had enough people mad at her already.

"Father, I'm hoping to do what I can to…make Finn smile again."

"Harumph," said her father.

"But I can't do that unless I can see him. I came to ask you for directions to Balmarran."

Osrik called for a car to take her there.

Balmarran estate lay a short distance beyond the small village of Skolvar, at the foot of a tiny mountain range called the Midlings. The estate was 130 kilometers from Lysgard—in American terms, roughly 80 miles. Liv sat behind the driver and stared out at the rolling countryside dotted here and there with rippling fields of grain and pastures full of fat-tailed sheep and tried to imagine what in the world she was going to say to Finn when she got there.

Silently she rehearsed a number of elaborate speeches. But in the end, she decided to wing it. She'd be honest and forthright and tell him she'd been thinking long and hard. And she'd decided she wanted to try to make a *real* marriage with him. She'd let the rest take care of itself.

The driver was no chatterbox. He stared at the road ahead of him and drove like Finn, faster than he should have. They roared around turns and more than once she had to ask him to please slow down.

It seemed no time at all before they reached Skolvar, where the houses were small and narrow, with steep-pitched dark roofs, each house painted a stunningly cheerful primary color—red, yellow or blue, with white window frames and shutters. The people stopped on the cobbled streets to smile and wave, as though they knew the black Mercedes must belong to their king, and they recognized Princess Liv in the back seat.

A mile or two beyond the village, the driver swung too fast around a curve and a castle loomed proud in the distance. She asked the driver and he confirmed that it was, in fact, Balmarran. Silhouetted against a cloudy sky, it was a long, imposing series of linked structures with a domed tower in the middle and more towers at either end.

"Skolvar granite, Highness," the driver gave out rather grudgingly when she asked him what kind of stone it was made of. "There's a quarry northwest of the village. Skolvar granite is famous for its pale, almost white color."

It truly was lovely, rising from the wooded grounds below it. It seemed more Georgian than medieval in style, more of a fine manor house, less a fortress. Arched windows ran the length of the two central buildings. They would let in lots of much-needed light during the long Gullandrian winters. It looked...gracious and welcoming. On a little grander scale than Liv preferred, but from here, well, it seemed a place she might be able to live.

And oh, she might as well face it. With Finn at her side, she could probably learn to live just about anywhere.

Trees obscured the view of the house as they got closer. And then they turned off the main road. A hundred yards later they arrived at an iron gate inset with medallions: dragons, their long tails twining in and out of some sort of runic symbol she didn't recognize. The pillars to either side were of that distinctive Skolvar granite.

The driver honked, but no gatekeeper appeared. With a put-upon sigh that Liv could hear even from the back seat, the driver got out and approached the gate. He fiddled with the latch, then grabbed an iron post on either side and gave it a hard shake. Nothing. He returned to the car.

"Sorry, Highness. The gate's locked up tight."

Liv got out her phone and dialed the castle. After an endless chain of unanswered rings, a machine finally picked up and invited her to leave a message.

Feeling ridiculous, she did. "This is Liv—Liv Thor...er, Danelaw. I'm at the front gate. Could someone please come down and let me in?" After that, she tried Finn's cell number. He didn't answer, so she left a message similar to the first one.

"Now what?" said the driver, looking put out, and remembering after a beat or two to add, with grudging respect, "Your Highness?"

"Now we wait."

The driver was not up for waiting. Not five minutes had passed before he announced that he didn't believe the iron fence could possibly run the entire perimeter of the estate. If she didn't mind, he'd find a way to get past it. He'd run on up to the castle on foot. In no time at all, he'd be back down with someone to open the gate.

Balmarran estate looked pretty big to her, and she doubted the man could have even passing familiarity with the layout. She sent him a disbelieving glance. "No time at all. Right."

"Highness, I don't mind confessing I've got a crack sense of direction and I'm real fast on my feet." He looked at her as if he'd go mad if he had to sit there and do nothing.

She accepted the fact that *she* might go mad if she had to watch him while he sat there and did nothing. She waved a hand at him. "Oh, all right. Leave the keys."

"Yes, Highness. Thank you, Highness." And he was off. He disappeared into the trees to the left of the road just as lightning flashed in the sky. Thunder boomed and fat raindrops began plopping on the windshield. Within seconds, it became a downpour. Liv figured the impatient fool would get smart and come back.

But he didn't. He was gone. And right then, as she stared at the gate, another man appeared just on the other side of it.

He wore a pair of soaked black pants, black boots and a dripping black-hooded slicker. He seemed to have materialized out of the storm itself. Liv was sure she hadn't seen him coming toward her down the driveway—and he had the hood pulled over his head, so she couldn't really see his face. He was perhaps six feet tall, and very thin.

The wonderful thing was, he had a key!

Liv scrambled over the seat as he unlocked the gate and walked each side wide open. He signaled her through and she started up the car.

When she got even with him, she rolled down the passenger window and leaned across to speak with him, though the rain gusted in over the seat, wetting the expensive leather and Liv as well. "Thank you so much."

He nodded. She could make out his face now, beyond the poor shelter of the hood.

Handsome in a gaunt, drawn way. And hardly more than a boy. Late teens, at the oldest. He shouldn't be out in this.

"You have shelter, close by?"

He only looked back at her—tongue-tied, perhaps deaf? Who could say?

She couldn't just drive off and leave him standing there. She pushed open the door and gestured at the seat. "Come on. Get in."

He backed off a step and turned his head sideways, like a wild thing scenting trouble.

She made her voice even firmer and waved him in. "I'm getting soaked here. Get in the car."

He hesitated a moment more and then he slid in beside her and pulled the door shut. Lovely. Water ran off him, pooling on the floor mat beneath his worn black boots, soaking the seat. He smelled like wet rubber from the slicker, and also like damp earth, kind of musky—not dirty, but not overly clean, either.

"Here." She reached for the dashboard controls.

"No need," he mumbled. "I'm not cold, milady."

She turned on the heater anyway. Warm air flowed in around her feet. The windshield was fogging up, so she switched on the defroster. Instantly the glass began to clear and she could see her way. She sent her soggy passenger a smile. "I'm assuming if I just take this driveway, we'll eventually end up at the castle. Is that right?'' He made a grunting sound. She decided to take it for a yes. ''And your name is…?''

''Cauley,'' he mumbled in the direction of his dripping shoes.

Cauley.

Of course. The wild boy, the groundskeeper's adopted son, the one whose heart Eveline had broken.

She felt a surge of pity for him. ''I'm Prince Danelaw's wife.''

He stiffened, shoved back his hood and stared straight at her then, pale gray eyes haunted looking, thin mouth unsmiling, wild, unkempt hair plastered to his thin cheeks. ''Prince Finn's new bride…'' He seemed far from pleased to make her acquaintance.

''Er, that's right. But tell you what. Just call me Liv.'' She held out her hand to him.

He didn't take it. ''Eveline hates you.''

Oh, terrific. ''Well, I'm sorry to hear th—''

Out of nowhere, his bony fist came at her, connecting squarely with her jaw. Liv's head flew back and hit the passenger window behind her.

She recovered, or at least, for a split second, she thought that she had. She sat up very straight and stared at the wild-eyed, wet boy in the other seat. ''What in the…'' She couldn't think how to continue.

The world was shifting, doubling up on itself, blurry and spinning. And then everything just faded away.

Chapter Seventeen

Finn sat in his study, watching the rain as it spattered the long windows. In spite of his dark mood, he couldn't help but admire the bright, ragged beauty of the lightning each time it forked down from the black rain clouds—Thor at his work, doing what a thunder god does best. The ensuing claps of thunder pleased him, too.

And yes. He knew he couldn't sit here staring out a window forever.

Action would have to be taken. And he knew what it would have to be.

He was no good without her.

She hadn't said she loved him, but she *had* wanted him to come with her. It would have to be enough for him. Tomorrow or the next day he would swallow his wounded pride and get on a plane bound for California.

He could live there.

He could live anywhere as long as she was there with him.

There was a discreet tap on the door. Without turning, he called, "Go away!" and continued watching the rain.

A moment later, the knock came again. Evidently, it was something he would have to deal with.

Wearily he stood. "Enter."

Mrs. Balewood, the housekeeper, stuck her head in. "So sorry to break in on you, sir."

"What is it?"

"There's a man at the side door, says he's Princess Liv's driver, that she's waiting, down at the gate. He says she called here to the house but got no answer. The man says she tried your cell phone, too. As to the house phone, I was down in the laundry. I didn't get to it and I—"

Finn waved an impatient hand. "Have you checked for a message?"

"I did. And it's there, sir. From your wife. She's down at the gate, just as the man at the door said."

He couldn't believe it. She was here. She had come to him. And this time he could think of only one reason for it: because here, with him, was where she wanted to be.

He felt the smile burst across his face. "Shouldn't Dag have let her in by now?" The groundskeeper's assistant wore a beeper on his belt. It went off whenever a vehicle pulled up to the gate.

"Yes, sir. Dag should have gotten to it."

Balder appeared in the doorway behind Mrs. Balewood. "What's afoot?"

"Liv's at the gate." He heard the buoyancy in his voice. It sounded good to his own ears.

"Wonderful." His grandfather beamed.

Mrs. Balewood was biting her lip. "Perhaps I should send a man down in a car to—"

As if he could wait for a servant to fetch her. "Get a car in front immediately. I'll do it myself."

The housekeeper was wringing her hands by then. "Sir. I feel there's something you must know...."

He scowled at her, impatient to be off. "Can't it wait?"

"Sir, your wife called yesterday. I told her you weren't to be disturbed. She insisted I fetch you to the phone. I was coming to speak with you, to see if you—"

He could hardly credit this. "You never said a word to me."

"Well, and I am so sorry, sir. You see, it was the young miss. She overheard me talking to the princess. She took the call and told your wife you didn't wish to speak with her. Then she told me to leave you in peace."

"Eveline," he muttered. "Why doesn't this surprise me?"

"The Norns curse the girl," his grandfather declared. "I'll have her hide."

"Good. And when you're done with her, I'll take a few strips off it myself." He turned to Mrs. Balewood. "That car. Now."

Liv groaned. The back of her head was pounding, her jaw ached and her neck had a terrible kink in it. She was wet, soaked through, and shivering. Also, there was something really wrong with her arms and her legs.

Carefully she opened her eyes. Nothing. The world remained pitch-black. She smelled earth, moist earth.

A cave?

How could she be in a cave? And the problem with her arms and legs...

They were tied, her hands behind her. She was gagged, as well—duct tape, it felt like. It went all the way around her head, so her hair pulled when she moved.

It came to her: the boy, the troubled boy. The one called Cauley, who loved Eveline.

She moved her aching jaw back and forth.

The boy had one hell of a mean right hook. Liv closed her eyes again—open or shut, she couldn't see a thing. She wished her poor head would stop pounding. Then maybe she could think clearly.

But then, maybe not.

Maybe thinking wouldn't be such a terrific idea. What was there to think about, really, except why Cauley had brought her here and what, exactly, he planned to do with her now that he had...and where was *here,* and how would she ever get out of here, out of the dark?

Finn.

She thought his name, and the sound of it in her mind was like a light, a bright, warm light going on in the endless dark, pushing back the shadows, making everything clear.

And her baby.

One single tear dribbled from the corner of her left eye and back into the hair at her temple, a little of it wetting the damp, mildew-smelling pillow beneath her head.

Her baby…

Lying here in this strange, cold cave of a place, trussed up tight, without a light, without a clue what might be about to happen to her, the reality of her baby came stunningly clear. A bone-deep shiver ran through her. She must get out of here, get to Finn. And above all, nothing—*nothing*—must happen to endanger her baby.

She tugged at the ropes. They were tight. Secure. But she would work at them. Maybe, with time, she could get them to loosen.

Was she alone in this place?

How could she know if Cauley might be sitting nearby, in the dark, just waiting for her to stir?

Well, fine. If he was lurking nearby, waiting for her to wake up, she'd give him what he was waiting for.

Madly, she grunted and groaned and writhed, lifting and dropping her head—though it made it ache even worse to do it—and her feet, too, pounding them against the mattress, making the springs beneath creak and groan.

Then, with a suddenness that stunned even her, she lay still, her heart beating as if it would burst from her chest, her breath tearing in and out through her nose.

Nothing.

A good chance, then, that she was alone.

Carefully she moved, testing the boundaries.

A single bed—definitely. Pitifully narrow, bucked up against a dirt wall on one side, the other dropping off into nothing. She straightened her legs all the way and felt the shape of a curved metal footboard. Inching upward, she felt the cold metal bar at the top. Judging by all the squeaking, it had to be an old single-spring bed.

So okay. She was on a dirty mattress on an ancient, narrow bed. That was something. That was...a boundary to push.

How long, she wondered, had she been unconscious? Had her driver reached the house? Did Finn know she'd been at the gate?

Oh, she had a hundred questions and no answers at all.

So maybe she'd do better to forget all the questions for now. Her job, right this minute, was to get loose and then try to find the way out.

She began wriggling her wrists, working to loosen the ropes. It took surprising concentration and effort, with her hands behind her, lying on one side. But that was a good thing—she felt warmer already, with the exertion. And her mind was on the task she'd set herself, not on what was going to happen when—and if—Cauley came back.

Or, maybe worse, what would happen if he never did.

As she worked at the knots, they did seem to loosen a little. Okay, it could be wishful thinking, but so what? False hope was a fine thing in a situation like this.

Her own weight on her left arm slowed her down. She rolled to her stomach, but that put her face into the pillow and made it hard to breathe. Plus, the pull of gravity at her shoulders and elbows made it all the more difficult to strain against the rope.

Grunting and huffing, she managed to wriggle her body, inching like a worm, squirming like a bug on a pin, until she reached a seated position, her back to the dirt wall beside the bed, her feet hanging over the other side of the mattress. Now she could lean forward or arch slightly against the wall. Either way, both hands were unencumbered by the weight of her torso.

She struggled for another measureless span of time, and then she saw the light. It was coming from a door-sized hole to her right, down in the corner, past the end of the bed.

The golden glow, growing brighter, allowed her to take quick stock of her surroundings: an earthen chamber, perhaps twelve by eight feet. There was a rough table beside the bed and a crude ladder-back chair against the dirt wall across from her. Another narrow tunnel led off into shadow a foot or two from the chair. In the far corner, she spotted some kind of crude gas heater, unlit, a coil of rope and a roll of silver tape beside it. A shovel and a rake. Tattered magazines and a candle—no matches, damn it—on the table.

The light grew brighter. Liv sat very still, waiting.

The light—an oil lamp—entered the room, with Cauley carrying it. He still had on that hooded slicker. It was wet, and he had the hood up. He stopped at the foot of the bed and regarded her. Water dripped from the slicker, plopping to the floor. The lantern light flooded upward beneath his chin, making his gaunt face look strange and ghoulish.

"You woke up," he said, looking vaguely bewildered, as if he'd doubted she'd ever regain consciousness.

She sat utterly still, her heart a drumbeat in her ears, and stared steadily back at him. It took all her considerable will to keep from grunting and squirming like a mad thing. Her dignity, at that moment, was all she had. And besides, she didn't want him to decide he ought to check the ropes he'd tied her with, possibly to tighten them even more.

He regarded her reproachfully, as if it was somehow her fault that he'd knocked her out and carried her here. "They're all looking for you," he said at last. "And for me, too, I got no doubt. Dag musta told them he sent me to open the gate."

Lifting a hand, he pushed back the hood. Suddenly he wasn't a ghoul anymore, just a very lost boy who'd done something rash that he deeply regretted.

He went and set the lamp on the table, then dropped into the chair across from the bed. "I don't know what to do now. It seemed the right thing, for a minute there. The right thing to do for Eveline. To nab you. She's mad because you made her brother sad. Eveline..." For a moment, he looked as if he might burst into tears. He stared down at the dirt between his battered boots. "She don't love me anymore. I had an idea that maybe she'd love me again if I made sure you were gone for good." He lifted his head then and looked across at Liv. "Why did you make the prince sad?"

And how was she supposed to answer that, with her mouth taped shut? She glared at him.

He grunted. "Well, I guess you ain't talking. Not

unless I take off the tape. And I guess I won't. I guess that wouldn't be so smart. I don't think they could hear you, if you screamed. But there's no need to take that chance.''

They stared at each other. In spite of the cold, Liv was sweating, clammy beneath the arms, wet at the hairline. She was absolutely terrified.

And determined that this poor, sick kid wasn't going to know it.

''And what now?'' he asked, eyes wilder than ever. ''What will I do now? They have to have figured it was me that took you—or if they haven't by now, they will, soon enough. I can't go back. I'll have to run away, I guess. Into the Midlings—or farther, all the way to the Black Mountains. Maybe the Mystics will take me in. Or maybe the *kvina soldars* will get me. They'll cut out my liver and string me up for the ravens to peck out my eyes.'' He stood. ''Oh, I don't know.'' He fisted a hand and punched it into his other palm. ''I just don't know…'' She ordered her body not to shrink back as he came close enough to pick up the lamp.

''I'll watch some more. See what they're up to. Then I'll be back.'' He started for the corridor beyond the foot of the bed, pausing just before he went through it. ''I'm sorry, but Eveline knows about this place. I brought her here once. They'll get it out of her, that I might come here. And that means they'll find you. You'll tell them what I did.''

She shook her head—fast, frantic.

But he only smiled, a sad, trembling boy's smile. ''Oh, don't lie. You know you will. There's only one way. And that's you dead and buried. And once that's done, I'll go far, far away.''

It was still pouring rain, but Finn had every man out. They were beating the bushes, systematically combing the grounds.

They'd found no sign of her other than the car, idling just inside the open gate, front doors open, her shoulder bag on the floor of the back seat.

He'd sent immediately for Dag and Dag had explained that he'd been helping one of the grooms in the stables. He'd dispatched Cauley to open the gate.

Cauley was nowhere to be found.

And Liv…

Finn stood in the rain by the abandoned car, his hair plastered to his face, water running down his nose. By the thousand roots of the guardian tree, if only he'd picked up the cursed telephone—four times, in total, she had called, twice to his cell phone, twice to the house.

And he'd been too busy pitying himself for loving her to answer.

If anything had happened to her…

He caught himself.

Nothing was going to happen. They would find her. She would be all right. It couldn't be otherwise. He wouldn't allow it.

The question was, why had she left the car?

It made no sense that she might have wandered off voluntarily. The gate had been opened, by Cauley, he was reasonably sure. The most logical move would have been for her to drive on up to the house.

It appeared, since the car was running, inside the gate, that she had started to do that.

What might have stopped her? Had someone lurking in the trees attacked her? An enemy of the king perhaps, set on kidnapping the king's daughter?

It was possible, he supposed. But it seemed something of a stretch. Laying an ambush would take forewarning and few could even know that she was coming here.

So what else could have happened? Was she lured from the car?

No. Not likely. If she'd left the car voluntarily, it seemed sensible she would have left the doors closed.

And come to that, why were *both* doors open? He leaned in on the driver's side. The rain had soaked the front seats by then. But there on the passenger seat floor: mud. Someone had been in that seat.

Cauley.

Yes. She could have ordered the boy out of the rain and into the car. That would be like her. She would do that.

And Cauley *was* missing, too.

Could he have dragged her from the car and carried her off? But why?

Finn ducked from the car and stood tall in the pouring rain.

Whatever the why of it, Cauley was the missing piece of this particular puzzle. If he found Cauley, he would find Liv, he could feel that in his bones.

But where to find Cauley? He'd already questioned Dag and both of the missing boy's adoptive parents. All three had said they didn't know. Finn believed them. Cauley's parents were frantic with worry. And Dag was simply puzzled.

Finn turned for the car he'd driven down from the house. It was time to have a little talk with Eveline.

Time did funny things, when you were in the dark, alone.

How long had it been since Cauley had left her? No way to know.

Liv closed her useless eyes and worked at the ropes. Her wrists were raw, but she hardly felt them. Only the blood, warm and sticky as it dripped into her palms, reminded her that she was injuring herself as she strained and struggled—minor injuries, of little consequence against the possible loss of her life and the life of her unborn child.

She worked at the ropes, pulling against them, out and then in, and then in a rubbing motion, back and forth. Really, the blood helped—it made her wrists slicker, and wet rope tended to stretch. If she only had time to…

Wait.

Yes!

Her right hand was almost to the point that she could…

Liv wriggled and pulled it, working it back toward her body, ignoring the burning pain as it abraded her already raw skin.

And it happened. Her hand came free.

She glanced furtively toward the place where Cauley had entered before. Nothing. Not the slightest glimmer of light. He wasn't coming yet. She brought her hands around to the front and started to rip at the tape—but no. Ankles first.

She hauled up her feet and put her blood-sticky hands to the task.

It was then that she saw the light.

Finn had sent his grandfather from the room. It was just the two of them, brother and sister, face-to-face.

"Eveline. I want to know. Where would Cauley go, if he didn't want to be found?"

Her gaze slid away.

He grabbed her by the shoulders. "Look at me. Tell me. I can see by your face that you know."

She squirmed against his grip. "Let me go." He held on, his fingers digging in. She cried out. "You're hurting me."

"And I'll hurt you worse. Freyja's eyes, you *will* tell me."

Eveline glared at him. "Oh, why are you so worried about her? You should be glad, if she's gone for good. You'll get over her. You'll be happy again."

He wanted to hit her—hard. Somehow he restrained himself. He settled on giving her a bone-rattling shake. "I won't be glad. I love her. It will kill me, if something's happened to her."

Eveline gasped. Then she scoffed. "No. That's not so.…"

"You know what happened to Father, when Mother died. Is that what you want? Your own brother dead?"

Those eyes—their mother's eyes—went wide. "No. No, Finn. I don't want that." He released her.

She staggered back. "Finn. I swear on our mother's name. I don't want that. And I don't want anything bad to happen to her, not really. I only want you not to be so sad."

He forced his voice to gentleness. "Then you must tell me. Where would Cauley go?"

The tears came then, twin trails of wetness down her satin cheeks. "He wouldn't hurt anyone. I'm sure he's only hiding. I know he—"

"By all the gods, Eveline. Where?"

She sobbed. Swallowed. And stood tall. "In the trees not far from the front gate. A tunnel he found beneath a shelf of rock. A tunnel that leads to a little cave. There's an old bed in there and a table and—"

He remembered. The safe-tunnels. There were three or four of them, at strategic places around the estate. His great-grandfather had had them dug at the time of the Nazi occupation. More than one Jewish Gullandrian had made use of them, to hide and later escape to freedom. He'd thought they'd all been covered over after the Second World War.

He grabbed his sister's hand. "Show me."

Together they ran for the door.

The light in the tunnel grew brighter.

Too soon!

No time to free her feet. She glanced in desperate longing at the shovel in the corner. No time to get to it.

Maybe the candle...

But what kind of weapon would that make?

She reached for her face, clawing, tearing at the tape. She yanked it down around her neck just as

Cauley appeared from the tunnel, his lamp in one hand.

And a knife in the other—a knife with a long, curved blade and serrations at the top ridge. A deadly-looking thing. He pointed it at her, his eyes narrowing as he saw that she'd almost managed to free herself. "Don't move. Don't make a sound."

He kept the knife toward her as he approached.

Liv resisted the urge to shrink back. She looked at him steadily, her limited options racing through her mind. Of course, she would fight. But how best to do that?

"Stop," she said. "Think."

He held the knife higher as he slid the lamp beneath his upraised arm and onto the table. "I said keep your mouth shut."

The hell she would. "You haven't done anything you can't come back from. Not yet."

"Quiet."

"No. Listen. Think. You know I'm right."

He swallowed, his Adam's apple bouncing hard. "I have to do it."

"No."

"I'm sorry…"

"You don't have to do this. You can stop. Stop right now."

"It's too late." Suddenly he was shaking.

"No, Cauley. It's not too late."

He raised the blade. It wobbled madly. His whole arm shook.

She saw the agony in his eyes and she knew. She was absolutely certain. He couldn't do it.

"Put the knife down, Cauley. You're no murderer, we both know you're not."

Tears glistened, pooled, spilled down the gaunt cheeks. "I...I don't know what else to do. You have to see, I don't have any choice."

She remembered something her mother had said a few days ago, when she finally told Liv why she'd left her father. And she recalled what Cauley himself had said earlier. "Yes. You have a choice. Something good can come of this."

He hiccuped, let out sharp moan. "Good? What good?"

"A chance for you—a way to a better life."

He sobbed, swallowed, swiped his nose with his free hand. And—oh, thank God—he lowered the knife. "A...chance?"

She nodded slowly, holding his eyes. "Take me to Finn. Now. Unharmed. And you'll go to the Mystics. I am the daughter of your king and I will make it happen. I swear it to you. The wise men beyond the Black Mountains will teach you how to live, how to...get along, in the world. It won't be easy. But in the end, you'll have a life, and a good one."

He was looking at the ground now, the knife at his side. She could have jumped him. She probably could have disarmed him. Maybe she should have.

But she knew in her heart it was already done.

His tears plopped to the damp earth between his battered boots. "I am nothing. Stupid. A gardener's boy."

"Cauley. Look at me."

Slowly he dragged up his ragged, wet head.

"Give me the knife. Now."

There was an endless moment when she doubted, when she feared she'd made a terrible mistake, the kind that would cost her life—and her baby's, too. But then he turned the knife.

He held it her way, handle out. She took it.

And that was when another light appeared from the passageway. They both froze.

Clearly, she heard it—pounding footsteps running toward them. The glow grew brighter.

Cauley spun for the other entrance.

"Don't," Liv commanded. "Stay. Face them. I will stand by you. It will be all right."

But the boy was already gone.

Chapter Eighteen

Finn burst into the small, dim space, his men behind him. He froze at the sight that greeted him.

Liv.

On her knees on a dirty mattress, a huge, swelling bruise on her delicate jaw, a loose cowl of silver tape around her neck, her ankles tied, a bracelet of rope on one bleeding wrist, bedraggled and muddy.

And holding a hunting knife.

"Oh, my darling," he whispered.

With a glad cry, she threw the knife to the floor and held out her arms to him.

It was all the invitation he needed. It took two steps to reach her. She surged up. He dropped the flashlight he held and grabbed her to him, tucking her head against his shoulder, rocking her, stroking her dirty, tangled hair. "It's all right, it's all right now."

"I know. Oh, Finn. I love you so."

It was all he'd ever wanted to hear. He kissed her hair. "As I love you. With all my heart."

She pulled back enough that she could look into his eyes. "I was coming to tell you. I want us to be together, any way you want it. Oh, Finn, I opened my morning gift. I found my panties. And I knew I didn't want them back. Not ever. You're the only man for me and I want—"

Tenderly he put a finger to her lips and whispered, "Shh. Wait." He gestured with a toss of his head toward the three gaping men packed tightly together at the foot of the bed.

"Oh. Sorry…" Shyly she tucked her head against his shoulder again.

Liv? Shy? It was a whole new side of her and it charmed him to his soul. He whispered in her ear, "Don't be sorry. We'll talk about it. In detail. Very soon. But now, I need to know…" She lifted her head and he demanded, "Who did this?" She looked away. By the runes, she actually seemed reluctant to say. He took her beneath the chin and made her meet his eyes. "I must know."

"Finn, he's just a boy. A confused boy."

His suspicions were confirmed. "Cauley."

She babbled on, excusing her kidnapper. "When he heard who I was, he got some wild idea he could earn points with Eveline by getting rid of me. He's young and hurt and angry and he didn't think it through. He simply acted, knocking me out, tying me up, bringing me here. But in the end, he couldn't hurt me."

He took her face in his hands. "Look at you.

Beaten and bloody. How can you say he didn't hurt you?''

"This was…a cry for help. Oh, Finn. Please. I want you to send him to the Mystics. I want—''

"He'll pay.''

"No. Don't hurt him. Promise me.''

"Where is he?''

She stuck out her black-and-blue chin at him. "Finn. I mean it.''

Where had that enchanting shyness gone? He wanted it back—or maybe not. By the tail of the dragon, he didn't care. Shrill or shy, he loved this woman, any way she chose to be. He grabbed her close again and muttered against her hair, "He hurt you and I'll have him dead. I'll see his severed head on a pike.''

"No. Please. Promise me.'' She clasped his shoulders and sought his eyes once more. "Promise. Don't hurt him.''

"Where is he?''

"Promise me.''

When she looked at him that way, what choice did he have? He muttered an oath beneath his breath and turned to his waiting men. "Capture him. Don't harm him. Bring him to me.'' He turned again to his battered, beautiful wife. "Well?''

She pointed at the far tunnel. "Through there. He ran out when he heard you coming.''

The men pounded off.

Liv slumped against him. "Oh, Finn. I hope your men obey you.…'' He said nothing. Wiser that way. She whispered in a broken voice, "I have missed you. And now that I've got you, I am never letting go.'' She lifted her poor, bruised mouth to him.

He claimed it in an endless seeking kiss.

''We can't stay in this hole forever, you know,'' he said several minutes later.

She snuggled closer. ''Why not? I could get used it—as long as you're here with me.''

''Very touching.''

She brushed her lips against his throat and tipped her dirty, blood-streaked face up, grinning. ''That's love for you.''

''But I think you should know...''

''What?''

''My sister's waiting outside.''

She wrinkled her patrician nose. ''All the more reason we should stay right here.''

He kissed her forehead. ''I promise you, Eveline is...much subdued. She's ready to apologize.''

''How strange. Is she ill?''

''No. Just very, very ashamed of herself.''

''As well she should be.''

''Don't hate her too much. She did keep me from learning that you called. But she had nothing at all to do with...this.''

Liv said softly, ''I know.''

''And maybe you'd like to get rid of that rope around your ankles?''

She took his face in her hands and planted one more kiss on his mouth—a hard, possessive one. ''Okay. Cut me loose.'' She dropped to her haunches, levered back and swung her feet out. And then she put her hand to the back of her head.

"Whoa. Got a bump here. A big one. It hurts." She looked around, her bright expression fading. "And you're right. Even with your sister waiting outside, I think I'd still like to get out of here. For a while there, I was afraid I never would."

He picked up the knife and cut the rope. Liv sighed. "Oh, that feels *good.*"

Her ankles were rubbed raw. He couldn't bear that. He threw the knife down and went to his knees in the dirt. Carefully, gently, he cradled one foot and then the other. He kissed each ankle, pressing his lips against the reddened flesh, wishing a kiss really could heal any wound.

"Ah," she said, as if his kisses had done exactly that. "Much, much better."

He looked up into her waiting eyes. "By all the gods, Liv Danelaw, we're going be so happy..."

Her mouth bloomed in a glowing smile. "Oh, Finn. I know it. I know we are. I understand now. This is the starting point. You and I. We make the future...together."

He had nothing to add to that. She'd spoken his thoughts exactly. He took his flashlight and blew out the lamp. "Come."

Hand in hand they went into the tunnel and together they made their way toward the light of day.

Epilogue

Liv's stalling had given Cauley a substantial head start. The men never caught up with him.

Two days later, he turned himself in.

Finn kept his promise to Liv and sent the boy north under armed escort, into the Black Mountains and beyond, to the Vildeland, where Cauley swore to submit to the tutelage of the Mystics.

Shortly after that, Finn and Liv—and Eveline—left for America. They'd decided to live there. After all, Finn could attend to his investments anywhere. They could pay frequent visits to Gullandria. And Liv had her dreams—dreams Finn meant to help her fulfill. She'd be back at Stanford in the fall.

They found a house not far from the university. It was going to be a challenge, with the baby coming. But they would manage. They had plenty of money, her mother and aunts and grandmother nearby to help out if they needed it. And most important, they had each other and so much love.

Eveline moved in with Ingrid, who had a way with strong-minded young girls. She welcomed another "daughter" in the house. Right away, Eveline's manners and attitude improved. She adored Ingrid. And she tolerated Hildy, who was tough and uncompromising and sometimes seemed to have eyes in the back of her gray head.

At the end of August, Ingrid threw a party in the backyard. She called it a wedding party—a wedding party for both of her newly married daughters. She said she wanted to make it up, a little anyway, to Liv and Elli, for missing the moment a mother should never miss: the moment when a daughter says her marriage vows.

It was a small gathering—family only. They tried to keep it low-key in hopes that the press wouldn't get wind of it.

Osrik appeared just before the two brides cut the matching tall white cakes. He'd wanted Liv and Finn to stay in Gullandria. But he was reasonably content with the way things had turned out. At least they were married in the truest sense now. They'd promised to visit him often—and to bring his grandchild.

Later in the afternoon, Elli took him aside and whispered in his ear that she'd been very sick that morning—she'd been sick and then she'd fainted. And yes, the Freyasdahl rash had appeared.

Osrik knew a deep happiness then. So much had

been lost. But life did renew itself. He looked across the backyard at his beautiful wife and he wished...

But Ingrid was cool to him, cool and never more than carefully polite.

Well, cool and polite was something, he told himself. A start, and a good one. A huge improvement, in fact, on all the years of bitter hatred.

Perhaps a healing had begun.

His one unmarried daughter stood off to the side. He winked at her.

Brit saluted her dad with her glass of champagne. She was happy for her sisters.

But her thoughts, really, were far away. In Gullandria. On a man she'd never met: the mysterious Prince Eric Greyfell, the man who, essentially, had started all this—the man her father had been scheming to get one of his daughters to marry.

Brit *had* been snooping, learning all she could about her lost brothers. Greyfell had been Valbrand's closest friend. From what she'd been able to learn, they were like brothers: blood-bound, as they said in Gullandria. To be blood bound meant that they had shared absolute loyalty, each to the other, loyalty until death.

Always, it had been understood that someday Valbrand would take the throne and Eric Greyfell would step into his father's shoes as Grand Counselor.

When Valbrand disappeared at sea, Eric had set off to find the truth about what had really happened to him. What had Eric learned? Brit wanted to hear it from Eric himself.

Her dad said the prince was in the Vildelund, with

the mystics, simple mountainfolk who lived, for the most part, by the old Norse ways. Her sources confirmed that. Greyfell was at home with the Mystics. His father, after all, had been born among them.

Brit set down her glass at the end of the cake table. Time to go. Back to Gullandria. Time to head for the Vildelund. Time to track down the elusive Prince Greyfell and find out exactly what he knew.

*   *   *   *   *

*Brit seeks the truth about her lost brother—
and finds a lot more than she bargained for in*

THE MARRIAGE MEDALLION.

*Coming in August,
only in Silhouette Special Edition.*

Beginning in May 2003 in

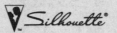

SPECIAL EDITION™

by **Christine Rimmer**

Three sisters, princesses all, foreign-born but California bred,
are about to rediscover their roots—and find love—at home.

In THE RELUCTANT PRINCESS (SE #1537) see Elli meet her
match in the king's warrior sworn to bring her safely home.

In PRINCE AND FUTURE...DAD? (SE #1556, August 2003)
be there as Liv marries her prince—even if he isn't the one her
father had in mind for her.

And coming in October 2003, watch as Brit finally hooks up with
the man who would be king in THE MARRIAGE MEDALLION.

**Viking Brides: Because every little girl is a princess—
and should marry her prince.**

Available at your favorite retail outlet.

Silhouette®
Where love comes alive™

SPECIAL EDITION™

WINCHESTER
BRIDES

A WINCHESTER HOMECOMING
Pamela Toth
(Silhouette Special Edition #1562)

Heading home to Colorado to nurse her wounds seemed like a good plan. But the newly divorced Kim Winchester hadn't counted on running headlong into her childhood sweetheart. The one-time rebel has become a seriously handsome rancher—the kind of temptation love-wary Kim would do *anything* to avoid.

Available September 2003 at your favorite retail outlet.

If you enjoyed what you just read,
then we've got an offer you can't resist!

Take 2 bestselling love stories FREE!

Plus get a FREE surprise gift!

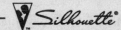

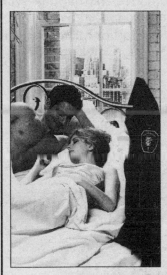

It's romantic comedy with a kick
(in a pair of strappy pink heels)!

Introducing

HARLEQUIN®

flipside

"It's chick-lit with the romance and happily-ever-after ending that Harlequin is known for."
—*USA TODAY* bestselling author Millie Criswell, author of *Staying Single*, October 2003

"Even though our heroine may take a few false steps while finding her way, she does it with wit and humor."
—Dorien Kelly, author of *Do-Over*, November 2003

Launching October 2003.
Make sure you pick one up!

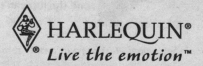

HARLEQUIN®
Live the emotion™

Visit us at www.harlequinflipside.com

SPECIAL EDITION™

MONTANA MAVERICKS

The Kingsleys

Nothing is as it seems under the big skies of Montana.

BIG SKY BABY
Judy Duarte
(Silhouette Special Edition #1563)

Pregnant and alone, Jilly Davis knew there was only one man she could turn to—her best friend, Jeff Forsythe. She needed his strong, dependable shoulder to lean on, but what she found in his arms was an attraction she couldn't ignore!

Available September 2003 at your favorite retail outlet.

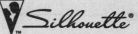

COMING NEXT MONTH

SPECIAL EDITION

#1561 HARD CHOICES—Allison Leigh
Readers' Ring
A night of passion long ago had resulted in a teenage pregnancy—specifically, the fifteen-year-old who now stood on Annie Hess's doorstep. Now, reformed wild child Annie was forced to confront her past…and Logan Drake, the man who had unknowingly fathered her child.

#1562 A WINCHESTER HOMECOMING—Pamela Toth
Winchester Brides
Kim Winchester returned home after a bitter divorce to find peace—not to face even more emotional turmoil. Seeing rancher and former childhood sweetheart David Major stirred up feelings in her that she'd rather not deal with…feelings that David wouldn't let her ignore….

#1563 BIG SKY BABY—Judy Duarte
Montana Mavericks: The Kingsleys
Pregnant and alone, Jilly Davis knew there was only one man she could turn to—her best friend, Jeff Forsythe. She needed his strong, dependable shoulder to lean on, but what she found in his arms was an attraction she couldn't deny!

#1564 HIS PRETEND FIANCÉE—Victoria Pade
Manhattan Multiples
Josie Tate was the key to getting firefighter Michael Dunnigan's matchmaking mother off his back. Josie needed a place to stay—and Michael offered his apartment, *if* she would help him make his family believe they were engaged. It seemed like a perfectly practical plan—until Josie's heart got involved….

#1565 THE BRIDE WORE BLUE JEANS—
Marie Ferrarella
Fiercely independent June Yearling was not looking for love. Her life on the farm was more than enough for her. At least before businessman Kevin Quintano walked into her life… and unleashed a passion she never thought possible!

#1566 FOUR DAYS, FIVE NIGHTS—Christine Flynn
They were stranded in the freezing wilderness and pilot Nick Magruder had to concentrate on getting his passenger, veterinarian Melissa Porter, out alive. He had no time to dwell on her sweet vulnerability—or the softness and heat of her body—as he and Mel huddled together at night….

SSECNM0803